WINTER
IN HIS

Winter In His

RICKY SMITH

Copyright © 2024 Heavenwar Publishing

Paperback First Edition

The moral right of Ricky Smith to be identified as the author of this work has been asserted in accordance with the Copyright, Designs and Patents Act of 1988.

All rights reserved. No part of this publication may be reproduced, distributed, or transmitted in any form or by any means, including photocopying, recording, or other electronic or mechanical methods, without the prior written permission of the publisher, except in the case of brief quotations embodied in critical reviews and certain other non-commercial uses permitted by copyright law.

Full cover arrangement and formatting by Ricky Smith. Various cover artwork elements licensed through Adobe Stock.

Interior artwork by Ricky Smith.

No Generative AI tools have knowingly been used in the creation of this work. All reasonable efforts have been made to ensure that licensed artwork is free from Generative AI content.

All enquiries via www.rickysmith.co.uk

First published 2024

ISBN: 978-1-0685793-0-1

For Adam,

The original Nusti, and without whom this story would still be waiting to be told.

CONTENTS

Map	10
Glyphs of the Faeries	11
Prologue: A Change on the Wind	13
1. Autumn's Awakening	19
2. White Forest	29
3. His Heart so Cold	35
4. A Faery's Purpose	41
5. Sleep, Little Ones	47
6. Lost in Winter	55
7. Reunited	61
8. Death in the Forest	69
9. That Joyous Hour	81
10. A Leaf out of Season	91
11. The Custodian	101
12. A Boy's Resolve	109
13. We'll Face it Together	115
14. The Hunter	121
15. A God Revealed	129
16. In Those Ancient Days	135
17. In His Winter	143
18. The World Beyond	155
Epilogue: A Change in Her Heart	159

ACKNOWLEDGEMENTS

It's something of a quiet joy to admit that this story came to me almost from nowhere. Those who read the original edition of A Line Unsundered that I published in 2020 will know that I had an entire world for that one book, and I'd originally intended to have a number of stories set across different worlds. Yes, I know it sounds very Cosmere, but I'm sure Brandon Sanderson would be gratified to know how much he inspires other authors.

I'd already decided to condense the universe of my stories into a single world in 2022 whilst I was busy writing another book during some time spent working in Bahrain, and that world had barely begun to form in my mind when I had a very particular conversation after I'd returned to the UK in November 2022.

I was talking with a friend about favourite seasons, colours, things like that, and somehow the conversation got to the point of me telling him that I could imagine him as an autumnal fairy. A little while later, the early premise of a story began to form in my mind around the character of a young fairy, who eventually became Nusti. As I began to pen some notes around this character, I realised that I really wanted this to be a cute little cosy fantasy, and that I wanted him to have a friend. Crina was born from that wish, and in the end the boys became two of my favourite characters that I've ever created. However, my friend Adam was undoubtedly the inspiration for both the initial character and the story, and so I owe him the biggest thank you of all for helping me to bring this story to the world.

As always, there's a tremendous group of people who give up their free time to read and review my work in its draft form. Huge thanks go to my Alpha Readers Kris and Jonny, who saw this book almost in its roughest form. To my Beta Readers Luke, Fran, Nick and Harley, thank you for putting up with my pestering. To my 'Street Team': Brittany, Elissa, Helen, Jack, River, and Ryan, who helped drum up interest on social media, thank you for your support. A book is never just its author: it's everyone who helped make it what it is. Thank you all for helping me to bring In His Winter to life.

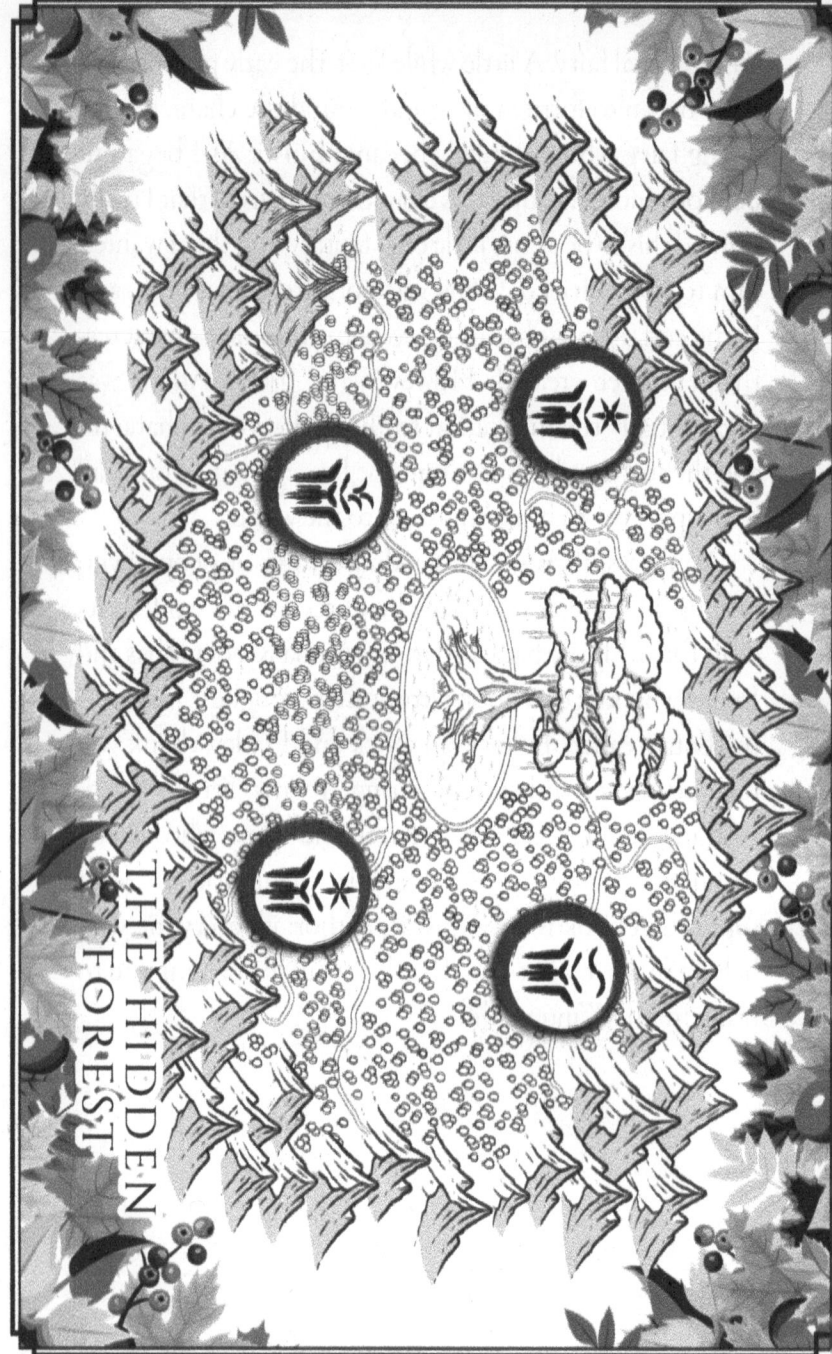

Vehleraelvir 'Life Faeries'
Keepers of Spring

Osaeraelvir 'Bright Faeries'
Keepers of Summer

Cuneraelvir 'Gold Faeries'
Keepers of Autumn

Luseraelvir 'Snow Faeries'
Keepers of Winter

1 Meleth vau am Esu

PROLOGUE
A Change on the Wind

THE RUSTLING WHISPER of countless ancient trees swaying in the wind washed over the faery as she gently held a single tree leaf between her delicate fingers. She smiled warmly as she regarded its changing colour, noting with familiarity the way that the margins had begun to yellow slightly, how they blended into the otherwise vibrant green hue that ran along the midvein and out across the lamina. Change was a constant in *Ainar'isil*, the Last Forest.

It was the same every year when Autumn arrived to herald the end of Summer, the long days of which had already begun to shorten. The leaves on the trees would begin to turn with the season, first from green to yellow, then yellow to burnt orange to red, turning the Forest into a realm of golden wonder before they finally fell to the ground as withered brown husks. They would blanket the floor of the Forest, decaying with the rains until they became little more than mulch underfoot. The snows of Winter would eventually cover them, leaving the Forest crisp and white until Spring came to bring new life to it once more.

The faery held out her hand and opened her fingers, allowing the leaf to float away on the morning breeze. It fluttered in the air for a few moments, as though enjoying the warm air currents, before falling to the Forest far below the great tree that she called home. The Thronetree afforded her a spectacular view of the canopies and the ring of mountains that surrounded them, though she couldn't see what lay beyond those towering peaks; she had surrendered that privilege a long time ago, back when the world had been bigger and her ambition had been grander. She had but one purpose these days, and though she often wondered whether it was enough, she knew she had no choice but to fulfil it.

Taking a deep breath, the faery closed her eyes and reached out with her mind. She sensed her connection with the Forest and embraced it, allowing its ancient energies to course through her; it felt right, natural, as though she were embracing a child of her own. She linked with the Forest most days, sensing the ebb and flow of the life within it, and allowing the magicks that sustained it to coalesce inside her. She was as much a part of the Forest as it was of her, and she took solace in the familiarity of the joining.

As she allowed the caress of the Forest to comfort her, she suddenly felt a chill run up her spine and out through the tips of her wings, shattering the harmony of the moment. It was a sensation she'd never felt before, and she quickly wrapped her arms around herself, rubbing them to try and banish the cold, unsettling feeling. As she struggled to identify the source of the discomfort, she realised it wasn't just inside her; the entire Forest had felt the disturbance. It was like some dark and alien presence had forced its way into her realm—something which didn't belong there. It was a violation; connected to the Forest as she was, the feeling left her unnerved and shaken, and she frowned in concentration and concern as she searched for the anomaly in the Forest's collective unconsciousness. Images of tree, beast and faery flashed through her mind, all of which had sensed the arrival of the intruding power.

Then it was gone, almost as suddenly as it had arrived and leaving no trace of its taint. Although the memory of it lingered, the faery felt perfectly normal again, just like she had moments before. She frowned, wondering what had just happened; there was no indication of where the strange presence had come from, but it had felt distinctly like something dark, something that stirred memories from an age long past. She reached out into the Forest once again and searched with her mind for some sign of whatever had disturbed her, but none was present. It was as though she'd imagined the entire thing, though she knew too intimately what it had felt like for it to be a fiction.

As the faery took a deep breath to calm herself, she decided not to dwell on it too much. A new season was arriving, and the *cuneraelvir*, the gold faeries, would soon be waking up. As the Keepers of Autumn, it was their time to watch over the Forest, and it was her responsibility to watch over them in turn. Whatever peculiarity had occurred just now, she would watch and wait to see what Autumn brought, whether it be answers or simply more questions.

IN HIS WINTER

Serunar a Meleth'hasha

CHAPTER ONE
Autumn's Awakening

IT WAS STRANGELY quiet as Nusti awoke, slowly opening his eyes to the world around him. His vision was blurry, as one might expect after being asleep for several months, and his eyelids felt extraordinarily heavy. As the chamber ceiling above him gradually came into focus, he welcomed the familiar sight of golden ivy hanging from the ancient stone above him, spreading like arteries across its surface.

The world had seemed quiet before, of course, in those years when Nusti had been amongst the first of his people to awaken from the Great Sleep. The awakening was never the same from one year to the next, and just once he'd been the very first gold faery to awaken, forced to wait several lonely minutes for the elders to rise and offer him guidance. This time, however, it was different; the quietness was heavy, oppressive, and altogether unsettling. It took several long moments for him to realise what the difference was.

It was utter, absolute silence.

There was no sound around him in the Chamber of the Gold Faeries. None of the usual noises were present, such as talking, the breathing of his waking siblings or the rustling of wings. Nusti turned his head to look at the wooden cot next to him—it was formed of a dense knot of vines and leaves that grew out of a tree stump in the rough shape of a bed. Asleep on it was one of the elder faeries, one whose name he couldn't quite remember, so he turned to the other side and saw the same thing: another sleeping faery, though this one he knew to be Beinel, one of the faeries from his own generation. The girl looked peaceful, and no closer to waking up than the elder faery on the other side of Nusti's cot.

As he sat upright and stretched, Nusti paused. There was no sign of movement from any of the other cots and, as he looked around whilst his wings spread for the first time in months, he realised that not one of the others had awakened. *This is wrong*, he thought. *At least some of them should be stirring already.*

A gentle rustling sound suddenly made his pointed little ears twitch, and he turned to see a small gust of golden leaves appear over his shoulder and hang in the air next to him. As it floated there, it took the form of a loose sphere slowing rotating in the air. The leaves gently brushed against each other, making a soothing noise almost like a whisper.

'Hello, friend,' Nusti said with a smile as he looked at his Nascent. 'Did you miss me?' The question was rhetorical: the creature couldn't answer him, though it spun faster for just a moment to show its own way of responding to Nusti's voice. His Nascent was, for all intents and purposes, a prenatal faery; a spirit of the Forest that was bonded to him. All faeries were bonded to a Nascent at birth, and the beings stayed with them for around a quarter century, experiencing the world with them and learning what they could of it. Eventually they would coalesce into a newborn faery, retaining much of the knowledge they'd learned during their nascence and allowing them to undertake their duties in the Forest with minimal delay. Nascents of Autumn typically took the appearance of a gust of leaves like Nusti's, though there were exceptions. Several of the other gold faeries had Nascents that appeared as balls of swirling dust, and another had one that took no physical form, but you knew it was close when you could hear the sound of distant chanting in your ear. Nusti had no idea what those of the other seasons looked like, however, though he enjoyed imagining what strange and wonderful forms they might take.

He swivelled on his cot and placed his feet on the ground, wiggling his toes as they sank into the soft amber moss that covered the floor of their sleeping chamber. It was always his favourite part of waking up each year, and he smiled as the familiarity brought him comfort. His Nascent bobbed back and forth in front of him, and Nusti brushed his hand along its side, lightly stroking one or two of its leaves. The little ball seemed to shiver in contentment as he did, then slowly moved away to investigate one of the other sleeping faeries.

Standing from his cot and stretching his wings again, Nusti turned his head from side to side as he carefully checked them over. He had always been proud of his wings, particularly the bold contrast between the black veins and edges, and the vibrant cells that gave them their distinctive gold and orange colour. They trembled and flicked as he stretched the muscles that controlled them, and he let out a contented little sigh; it felt good to move them again after a long sleep.

That was the other thing that bothered Nusti: he couldn't quite shake the feeling that he'd slept for a lot longer than usual. Such a thing was impossible, of course, but he certainly felt groggier than he normally did when waking up. Perhaps the elders would have a view when they awoke; they were certainly the wisest amongst his people, and though he'd never heard of a faery having trouble emerging from the Great Sleep, if anyone would know it would be them. *If they ever wake up*, he thought, stepping away from his cot.

Nusti strolled through the chamber for a short while with his Nascent in tow, passing by various cots full of his sleeping brethren. The little ball of leaves occasionally moved curiously towards one or other of the faeries, but always returned before Nusti got too far. Not one of them showed signs of stirring and, as the minutes went by, he felt himself beginning to panic. No faery had ever been awake on their own for this long before, and he wasn't yet old enough to know what he should do in a situation like this. There should have been elders and wardens awake to take charge, but there was nobody. He was all alone, and he needed help.

Making his way to the centre of the chamber, Nusti approached the cot of their leader. Harees was the oldest of all the gold faeries and was usually one of the first to awaken. He, however, was slumbering just as peacefully as all the others, blissfully ignorant of Nusti's growing concern. The boy frowned. *What's going on here?* he thought. *Why isn't anyone waking up?* He reached out tentatively with his hand towards Harees, wondering for a moment if he would get in trouble for trying to wake him but shook his head as he dismissed the concern. Nobody was waking up, and if he didn't do something about it then Autumn itself could be at risk.

Placing his hand on Harees' shoulder, Nusti shook him gently. Harees didn't stir, so Nusti rocked him a little harder, still without success. His Nascent floated down to form a sort of crown around Harees' head, and Nusti wondered if it was somehow trying to communicate with the old faery. Harees, however, didn't react at all to his new headwear, and eventually Nusti decided to risk the elder faery's wrath and shook him as hard as he could.

Harees remained sound asleep, and Nusti felt himself beginning to panic. If he couldn't wake Harees or any of the others, it meant something had gone very, very wrong. Had something happened whilst they'd been asleep? Had the bright faeries managed to end their watch on Summer, or were they being kept awake because his own people couldn't stir from their slumber?

The questions buzzed in Nusti's mind as he slumped down on the floor against Harees' cot, allowing his head to roll back against the gnarled bark of the tree stump that formed its base. He felt so helpless, and there was nobody he could turn to for guidance or reassurance. His eyes moved to one of the small windows high up on the far side of the chamber, looking to the sky outside. That too seemed out of the ordinary; the colour was off, and there was something else out there too; what looked to Nusti like small, white leaves seemed to be falling from the sky. He had never seen anything like them before, and they added to the mystery of his situation.

Letting out an exasperated sigh, he clambered to his feet and rubbed the back of his neck as he looked around once more. He wasn't finding any answers here, and with no way of waking the others he was at a loss for what to do next. It seemed the only sensible thing to do was venture out into the Forest and try to fulfil his duties whilst investigating why the others hadn't awoken. Before that, however, there was a rite he needed to perform.

As he made his way to the vast open space in the centre of the chamber, he regarded the great tree that stood at its centre. Each of the four faery chambers supposedly had their own tree, though their appearances differed as they were eternally locked into the state of the season they were bound to. The *Isi a Meleth'hasha*, the Tree of Autumn, was perpetually covered in golden leaves, and the soft amber moss that grew across the floor of the chamber crept partway up its trunk. Nusti always liked to imagine that, like him, the tree just wanted to keep its roots warm.

The rest of the trunk was dotted with tiny pupae—the larval form of the faeflies that all faeries became when their lives drew to an end. They were almost visually indistinguishable from normal butterflies, other than the fact that they emitted a soft, white light. The pupae emitted that same light, causing the trunk to glow gently. Nusti glanced over them in silence, wondering what it would be like to spent the rest of time in that form; faeflies were immortal once born, and they never slept again. Once reborn, a faefly simply joined the rest of the creatures in the Forest, their eternal waking state allowing them to experience all the seasons instead of just the one they'd been bound to as faeries.

Returning his attention to the empty space in which he now stood, Nusti began a series of carefully practiced movements that stretched the various muscles in his body. Some involved his arms, others his legs and a few required him to flex his wings with utmost precision. The *Athel a Serunar*, the Dance of Awakening, was an ancient practice used by the faeries to fully awaken their minds and bodies after spending three quarters of the year asleep. It had been used since the first days of the Forest, and Nusti found it helped him to focus for the coming months. The Dance was usually led by the olvuhr, the singer of each faery race, whose duty it was to lead the faeries out into the Forest again. However, like the rest of the gold faeries, their singer was sound asleep.

It was a strange feeling for Nusti. The faeries and their Nascents usually danced together, moving in perfect unison to the words sung by the singer as they warmed up their bodies for the season ahead. However, Nusti was alone this time except for his own Nascent, and whilst he knew the movements, the Dance felt somewhat underwhelming and empty without his people around him and the music of the singer in which to lose himself.

Despite his uncertainty, Nusti continued the Dance until it reached its crescendo, at which point he leapt into the air, fluttering his wings so they held him aloft as his Nascent formed a wide, scattered ring and slowly rotated around him. From his elevated position, Nusti gazed out over the chamber. Five hundred cots were arranged in concentric rings around the space in the centre of the chamber, each with a single faery asleep on it. The sight of four hundred and ninety-nine faeries all sleeping soundly was truly special, but he once again found himself wondering what was keeping them in slumber. He'd never heard of any of the four faery races failing to wake at their appointed time, be it in history or in legend. This was unprecedented, and he knew he needed to find out more.

Alighting on the floor, Nusti took one last look at Harees before heading for the entrance to the chamber, his Nascent weaving playfully between his legs. He had no idea whether he would find what he was looking for outside, but he was left with little other choice. Nobody else was stirring, and he'd run out of other ideas. Reaching the great door, he placed his hand on it and was surprised to find that it was cold. With Summer only just ending, it should have been comfortably warm.

Come to think of it, Nusti thought, *the entire chamber has had a chill to it.*

As a suspicion grew in his mind, he pushed the door open and took a single step into the outside world before he froze, his eyes widening in shock. The Forest was white, and a bitter chill in the air told him everything he needed to know. This wasn't Autumn.

He'd awoken in Winter.

Vir Isil

CHAPTER TWO
White Forest

NUSTI STOOD IN the entrance of the chamber in absolute silence as the reality of his situation slowly sunk in. It was Winter. Winter! He was awake out of season, in a strange world that he didn't recognise. The freezing cold air made his chest hurt, and he braced himself on the doorway as he struggled to breathe. He could feel anxiety rising in his stomach as his breathing quickened despite the cold making it difficult, and he closed his eyes to try and focus.

It's alright, he told himself as his Nascent coiled around his braced arm. *It's still the same Forest. It's still the same trees. It's just a different season, that's all.*

Slowly opening his eyes again, Nusti felt his breathing

return to normal as he took in the majesty of the world around him. It seemed like an entirely different place to him now, as he had never seen the Forest in Winter before. All the yellows, oranges and reds of Autumn were gone, replaced by a landscape of pure white snow that was broken only by the occasional glimpse of brown soil or tree bark. Many of the leaves were gone, leaving a host of trees with dark, scant branches as far as the eye could see.

It was also bright, far brighter than what Nusti was used to in Autumn. The sunlight reflected off the snow and ice, and he had to squint to make out any detail against the glare in his eyes. He recognised the placement of trees, rocks and other features, but he had to concentrate hard to do so. It was surprising to him how the change in colours could make the world look and feel so different.

A rustling sound from a nearby cluster of bushes drew his attention, and Nusti turned to see a small, white fox emerge into the open. It sniffed about for a moment, then paused as it noticed him. Repressing the urge to approach it, Nusti simply stood and watched as the fox tilted its head slightly, regarding him with piercing azure eyes before trotting away into the undergrowth. His Nascent made as if to follow it but stopped short of entering the bushes, apparently thinking better of the pursuit.

Nusti was familiar with most animals of the Forest that appeared in Autumn, but he knew well enough that there were those that only appeared in the other seasons.

That hadn't stopped the sight of a fox with brilliant white fur and blue eyes taking him slightly by surprise, however. Unnerved as he was by being awake on his own, he was even more nervous about what else lay outside the chamber at this time of year. It was not his world, and other faeries ruled the Forest at this time. He knew nothing of the *luseraelvir*, the snow faeries, and seeing as they knew nothing of his people in return, they might not take kindly to a strange faery from another season walking amongst them uninvited. *Even if it's not my fault that I'm awake*, Nusti thought.

As he made his way carefully through the Forest, he wondered what other creatures of Winter he might encounter. It wasn't just the animals that were strange to Nusti; much of the foliage was different as well. Stopping by a small tree, he reached out to pluck one of the large berries that was growing on its branches. He knew this tree, having spent many days sitting under it as he tended to his charges, but he'd never seen it bearing fruit. The berry was perfectly round, with a blue skin much like that of the fox's eyes. He sniffed it cautiously, then took a small bite from it.

A sensation almost like fire washed over his tongue; whilst not unpleasant, it was unlike anything he had tasted in Autumn. Berries in his season tended to be warm and sweet; he found the flavour of this one to be rich and spicy, as though it were cultivated to make whoever ate it feel warmer somehow. His Nascent had been cautiously touching the berry with the tip of one of its leaves as though interested in trying it too, though it wasn't capable of eating food itself. Not wanting to waste the gift of the Forest, Nusti popped the rest of the berry into his mouth and munched happily as he wandered off towards a stream that he knew was nearby.

After a few minutes of fighting his way through the frozen undergrowth, which had involved being covered by several unexpected showers of snow as he'd pushed branches aside, Nusti came to the stream. As he looked at the water, he suddenly realised he was desperately thirsty from his prolonged sleep. As he knelt down and dipped his hand into the stream, he immediately pulled it out with a gasp as he was hit by the shock of how cold it was. He wiped his hands on his trousers, then rubbed them together to try and warm them up. Even more unbelievable to Nusti was the sight of fish swimming through the stream. *How can they live in such cold water?* he thought.

His Nascent suddenly dove into the stream, circled underwater for a few seconds, then emerged; its leaves shivered slightly, as though it was trembling from the cold. Nusti chuckled and shook his head as the Nascent coiled around his waist for warmth. There was so little he understood about Winter, which made his being awake in it all the more uncomfortable. He realised that he must have slept through the entirety of Autumn, but if that was the case then why hadn't the others been able to wake him up as normal? Was he sick? Would his sleep cycle be disrupted forever? The questions danced through his mind as he watched the fish swim lazily along the stream; his Nascent had returned to investigate and was now following them just above the surface of the water. He was so distracted by his worries that he didn't hear someone slowly approach him from behind, their footsteps making no sound in the snow and frost.

'Who are you?'

The voice was quiet but direct, and Nusti spun round in surprise to see who had spoken. In front of him stood a boy about his own age, with white hair, pale skin, and piercing blue eyes that seemed to bore right through him.

A snow faery.

Airi Cruhn umar Lusa

CHAPTER THREE
His Heart so Cold

THE TWO BOYS stood looking at each other for several moments, each unsure about the other. Nusti regarded the boy that was standing in front of him with a mixture of awe and trepidation; he was the first snow faery that he'd ever seen, and he had little idea of what to expect from him. The boy's hair was pure white, with a long fringe that fell across his forehead, unlike Nusti's own curly brown hair which stuck out in all directions. His eyes, which were regarding Nusti with a cold look, were a bright, icy blue which contrasted with his pale, perfect skin; there was a similar contrast on his hands, where his fingers were tipped in blue fingernails. His wings were similar in shape to Nusti's, though unlike his gold and orange ones, the other boy's had white cells that bled into pale blue. He was dressed in a mix of white and blue clothing with intricate silver adornments, including a pair of delicate silver bracers and a single snowflake earring in his right ear.

'Who are you?' the boy asked again, and Nusti swallowed nervously. His Nascent hung behind him, clearly sensing his anxiety as it hovered by his shoulder. The boy looked at it briefly, his eyes flashing as he recognised it as a Nascent, but he switched his intense gaze back to Nusti almost immediately. He wondered for a moment where the boy's own Nascent was, but assumed it might simply be hiding nearby. How would it interact with his? What did Winter Nascents even look like?

'I'm Nusti,' he replied eventually. 'What's your name?'

'You're not one of us,' the boy continued, ignoring Nusti's question. 'Why are you here?'

Nusti frowned at the boy's refusal to tell him his name but decided it would be best not to antagonise him. After all, he was in an unfamiliar season, with none of his own people to turn to for help. It wouldn't go well if he caused trouble, and there was every chance that he might have to seek help from the snow faeries.

'I don't know,' he said eventually. 'I only just woke up, and I don't know why I'm awake in this season. I'm really confused about what's happened.' He paused briefly, considering the other faery. 'Would you tell me your name? I'd really like to know.'

IN HIS WINTER

The boy narrowed his eyes as he pondered Nusti's request. 'Crina,' he said eventually. 'My name is Crina.'

'It's nice to meet you,' Nusti said with the slightest of smiles. 'I've never met a snow faery before. I suppose you've never met one of my kind either.'

'No,' Crina replied, 'and I don't know if it's nice to meet you or not. I don't know you, and you shouldn't be here. This isn't your season.'

'I know,' Nusti said, 'but—'

'You're cold,' Crina interjected. Nusti looked at him, blinking in confusion before realising he was shivering, unacclimatised as he was to the snow and ice. The other boy unclipped a white cloak from around his shoulders and held it out towards Nusti at arm's length. 'Here,' he said, 'take it.' His words were direct, and hardly suggested concern for Nusti's wellbeing.

When he didn't move immediately to take the cloak, Crina rolled his eyes and tossed it to the ground at Nusti's feet. 'Take it or don't, it's up to you,' he said as Nusti's Nascent slowly investigated the garment, arranging its leaves to spread out across the material. Crina's tone was flat, seemingly empty of any emotion, and Nusti wondered if this was how all snow faeries behaved. His own people were hardly the most joyous; being the custodians of the Forest when it was dying, they were prone to melancholy, but they still had their emotions. Crina, on the other hand, seemed to lack any emotion at all except frustration, and it made Nusti immensely uncomfortable. Determined to try and make a friend, however, he smiled at the boy.

Visibly unsettled by this gesture, Crina wheeled about on his heel and stalked off into the Forest. Nusti hurriedly stepped forward and picked up the cloak, wrapping it around himself as he hurried after the other faery. It was exceptionally warm, with a fur collar that tickled his neck.

'Wait!' he called out, darting around trees and bushes to catch up with Crina. The snow faery stopped and turned to look at him.

'What do you want?' he demanded.

'Can I come with you?' Nusti asked, slightly out of breath from chasing him.

Crina narrowed his eyes again. 'Why?'

'I have nowhere else to go right now, and I need to find out why I'm awake out of my season. You were kind to me by giving me your cloak, so I figure you're my best chance for staying safe and finding some answers.'

'And how do you intend on finding answers?' Crina demanded. 'I don't have any for you; I've never heard of someone being awake out of season.'

'I don't know,' Nusti admitted. 'Perhaps your elders could help?'

Crina snorted. 'Good luck. They won't help an outsider.' Then, more quietly, he said 'they barely even help their own.' He looked away, and Nusti thought he saw a flicker of emotion cross Crina's face.

'Well, I'd still like to come with you,' he said quietly as he looked at the other boy hopefully.

Crina looked at him, then made a small noise of irritation in his throat. 'Fine,' he said plainly, 'but don't get in my way.' He strode off again, leaving Nusti to follow close behind with the cloak wrapped tightly around his shoulders. As he beckoned for his Nascent to follow, Nusti looked ahead at Crina. *Please let him lead me to help*, he thought.

Drey a'i Eraelvir

CHAPTER FOUR
A Faery's Purpose

AS THE TWO boys walked through the snow-covered Forest, Nusti quickly began to suspect that he wasn't welcome. Crina moved swiftly, never slowing or checking to make sure Nusti was keeping up. Though keen to make sure he didn't get in Crina's way as he'd asked, Nusti was finding it increasingly difficult to keep the gap between them from increasing. The Forest felt unfamiliar to him, and he occasionally found his footing was uneven as he trudged through the frozen undergrowth. He noted that there was still no sign of Crina's Nascent; was it still hiding, and how had it managed to keep up with them?

Deciding he might be able to slow Crina down through conversation, Nusti dodged a low hanging branch and hurried up alongside the other boy. 'Crina?' he asked, slightly out of breath. 'Can I ask you something?'

'You just did,' Crina replied, sounding less than interested in answering Nusti's questions.

'I suppose that's true,' Nusti said with a chuckle. 'Alright, I'd like to ask you another question then.' *There*, he thought, *that wasn't technically a question.*

'Get on with it,' Crina said in his stony voice.

'I was wondering,' Nusti said quietly, 'where's your Nascent?'

Crina stopped dead in his tracks, and Nusti saw his fists clench as the other boy turned to face him. He wore a mixed expression of anger and frustration, and Nusti shuffled his feet nervously as his Nascent clung to his side.

'That's none of your business,' Crina replied from behind gritted teeth.

'I'm sorry,' Nusti said apologetically. 'I didn't mean to upset you.'

'It doesn't matter whether you meant it or not,' Crina said. 'It's nothing to do with you. Don't ask me again.'

Nusti looked at him in confusion. Why was he so upset? What had happened to his Nascent? 'I'm sorry,' he said again.

'And stop apologising!' Crina snapped. 'People always apologise for things when they don't mean it. They should just say what they think and if the other person doesn't like it then that's *their* problem.' He turned and headed into the

Forest once more, with Nusti following him as he stormed through the trees. The boys walked in awkward silence for a few minutes, and Nusti felt his Nascent brush up against his arm slightly. It did it a few times, as though nudging him in encouragement.

'So, what's your duty in the Forest during Winter?' he asked, hoping to steer the conversation onto a friendlier course. When Crina didn't reply immediately, Nusti wondered if he'd lost his chance to talk. However, a few moments later the other boy sighed, briefly glancing back at Nusti as his walked, his pace slowing ever so slightly.

'I look after animals,' Crina replied shortly, continuing to head deeper into the Forest. Nusti waited for him to continue, but he said nothing further as they walked.

'Which ones?' Nusti asked excitedly, probing a little for more information. 'I look after the smaller animals; you know, the ones that sleep all through Winter.'

Crina continued on, not breaking stride or slowing down this time. 'I care for the deer,' he replied, then paused before adding 'particularly those that are starting to lose their antlers.'

Nusti stopped in his tracks. 'What?' he asked in shock as his Nascent laid across his shoulders.

'I look after deer,' Crina said again, rather matter-of-factly.

'I heard that bit,' Nusti said excitedly. 'What do you mean about them losing their antlers?'

It was only then that Crina looked back and realised Nusti had stopped following him. 'You don't know?' he asked, narrowing his eyes at Nusti. 'Deer lose their antlers towards the end of Winter, and they regrow each year.'

Nusti was stunned. He saw the deer with their glorious antlers in Autumn, but never thought they could actually lose and then regrow them. What else didn't he know about the creatures that inhabited the Forest? What happened to the ones he cared for?

'What other animals appear only in Winter?' he asked. 'I saw a fox earlier—are there any more like that?'

'Plenty,' Crina replied, annoyance creeping into his voice. Though Nusti sensed the other boy was growing tired of his questions, it occurred to him in that moment that Crina would never have seen the animals that he looked after. Mice, squirrels, badgers...all were asleep whilst Crina was usually awake.

'I have an idea,' Nusti said. 'What if I show you some of *my* creatures?'

'Why?' Crina frowned.

'Because you've never seen them before,' Nusti replied. 'They're always asleep by the time you wake up, so I thought it would be nice to show you.'

'I don't know.'

'What's the harm? Aren't you curious?'

Crina shrugged. 'I suppose so. None of the deer will have started to lose their antlers yet, so I can't show you what they look like without them, and I don't have anything better to do right now. I suppose it couldn't hurt.'

'That's amazing,' Nusti replied with a smile. 'Let's go!' And with that he dashed off towards a familiar cluster of trees further down the path, with his Nascent fluttering around him and Crina following behind with a less than enthusiastic look on his face.

Ishal, Imir

CHAPTER FIVE
Sleep, Little Ones

A SHORT WHILE later, Nusti carefully pulled back a section of frozen brush underneath a tree that he knew to be a favourite nesting spot for a particular group of animals. He quietly checked inside the burrow, his Nascent circling the entrance at a respectful distance. Sure enough, whilst it was dark inside, he could just about make out the forms of several forest mice curled up together for warmth, their little bodies swelling ever so slightly as their shallow breathing continued through their long sleep. Nusti smiled; he always made sure to see all of his charges off to their Winter rest, but so rarely did he get time to check in on them before he was recalled to his chamber for the Great Sleep.

Turning to look over his shoulder, he silently beckoned for Crina to approach with an encouraging wave. The snow faery cautiously stepped forward and dropped to his knees beside Nusti, craning his neck to peer inside the burrow, at which point Nusti was surprised to hear a quiet gasp exit Crina's mouth. The other boy had been somewhat stoic thus far, and he'd wondered if the mice might only be of limited interest to him. The little burst of expressive surprise from Crina brought a smile to Nusti's face, though he was careful not to let the other boy see it—he didn't want to risk upsetting him again.

'They look so peaceful,' Crina whispered as he leant in a little closer, carefully bracing himself against one of the roots of the tree so as not to fall in.

'I know,' Nusti replied. 'All cosy and warm in their little hidey-hole.'

'I've never seen such a thing,' Crina said, frowning slightly.

'Surely some of your deer must sleep in the winter?' Nusti asked.

'Yes, but...' Crina paused. 'These are different. They look so small and helpless.'

'Not helpless,' Nusti replied. 'You look after the deer, right? Surely there must be one of your people who cares for the mice whilst they sleep?'

'Possibly,' Crina said with a shrug. 'I don't really pay attention to what the others do.' He looked back inside the burrow. 'Do you suppose we look like that when we sleep?'

'Absolutely!' Nusti exclaimed before lowering his voice; it wouldn't do to disturb the mice. 'When I'm one of the first to awaken,' he continued, 'I often take a walk amongst the others and watch them sleep whilst we wait for them to wake up. It was like that when I woke up this time, but I was the only one. It's the same when it's time to enter the Great Sleep; I'm often one of the last to return and usually see the others already settled down.'

Crina frowned slightly and clambered to his feet, taking care not to make too much noise. 'I see,' he said quietly as Nusti leaned closer to the burrow.

'Sleep, little ones,' he whispered, before covering the burrow back up and standing to face Crina. 'What's wrong?' he asked, noticing the pensive expression on the other boy's face as he stood. Crina was silent for a moment, before turning to look at Nusti.

'I've never seen my own kind sleeping,' he said eventually. 'Every year, without fail, I'm always the last to awaken. The others vary as to how soon they rise and slumber, but for me it's always the same.' He paused, pushing his fringe to the side. 'I also choose to sleep before the others,' he added.

'Why?' Nusti asked.

'I just don't see the point in being awake longer than I have to,' Crina replied. 'Once my duty is done, why not just go back to sleep?' He had a look somewhere between confusion and sadness on his face, as though he'd struggled with this truth for a long time, and Nusti felt a stab of pity; it was the first time since meeting Crina that he'd had seen any sign of deep emotion from the snow faery. As his Nascent circled them slowly, Nusti remembered that he still didn't know about Crina's Nascent. He decided, however, that it wasn't the right time to press that particular issue. Whilst Crina's frustration had been stifled, he suspected the other boy was still suppressing far more complicated feelings.

'I don't know what to say,' Nusti said softly. 'None of our kind have ever been affected in such a way. We all vary as to when we rise and sleep.'

'"Our kind",' Crina replied with a snort. 'We're all faeries, all of us. But we act like the faeries of the other races are strangers, like we're separated by more than just our seasons.'

'Aren't we?' Nusti said, considering the divisions between the four groups of faeries. 'We look completely different, Crina, right down to our fingernails.' He looked down at his own, which were amber in colour. 'We never meet each other, and we're forbidden to enter any other sleep chamber in the Forest. Each group rises and sleeps with its assigned season; the first snow faery rises when the last gold faery sleeps; that's the way it's always been.'

'What's your chamber like?' Crina asked suddenly. The sudden curiosity of the white-haired boy took Nusti by surprise, and he stared at Crina for a few seconds. As though he believed he'd crossed a line, albeit one of his own making, the boy suddenly shook his head. 'I'm sorry, I shouldn't have asked.'

'No,' Nusti said quickly. 'It's alright. It's just that's the first time you've shown any interest in me or where I come from. It's nice to see.'

Crina stood quietly, staring at the ground. 'It's...hard for me,' he said eventually. 'I don't speak to many other faeries normally. Certainly not a faery from another season.'

'Well, you're talking to me now.' Nusti grinned, a mischievous idea forming in his mind. 'Say, what would you say to taking a peek inside the gold faeries' sleeping chamber?'

'What?' Crina stared at him, then shook his head. 'No. No, no, it's forbidden.'

'What's the harm?' Nusti asked. 'All of my people are asleep, and nobody else is in there.'

'It's not allowed.' Crina's voice was flat once more, as though the feeling that had briefly crept into it had disappeared.

'Please?' Nusti pleaded, a sick feeling growing in his stomach as he sensed Crina withdrawing again. 'Then... maybe you can show me where you rest?' He stepped towards Crina and offered his hand, but the other boy stumbled away and shook his head. His eyes were wide, almost as though he were afraid of Nusti.

'It's against the rules!' Crina hissed. 'Why are you trying to make me break them? You shouldn't even be here; you should be asleep.' He turned to walk away, and Nusti reached out for him.

'Wait, Crina! Please?' He felt his bottom lip tremble, but he fought back the tears in case Crina saw; he'd proven he wasn't entirely comfortable with overt displays of emotion.

The other boy didn't look back, however. 'Just leave me alone,' he said coldly, before spreading his wings and taking off into the Forest, leaving Nusti stood alone to wonder what he'd done wrong as his Nascent weaved playfully amongst the flakes of snow that fell silently around him.

IN HIS WINTER

Aisvre u Ihlais'hasha

CHAPTER SIX
Lost in Winter

SEVERAL LONG, COLD days passed as Nusti walked dejectedly through the Forest on his own, with Crina's cloak pulled tightly around his shoulders for warmth. It seemed a stranger place since Crina had left him, and though he hadn't known the other boy for very long, Nusti was feeling his absence more keenly than he'd expected. Even the presence of his Nascent, which was usually able to cheer him up with its innocent, playful nature, did little to ease his sense of isolation and loneliness.

Nusti's experience of Winter thus far was proving to be a thoroughly miserable one. The unfamiliarity, the loneliness, all of it was threatening to overwhelm him. He'd wandered day and night through the Forest, visiting those places where he usually spent most of this time. Some had been familiar to him despite the snow, but others had seemed so different that he'd lost his way several times.

He'd had countless hours to think about what had happened between him and Crina, and as he went round and round in his mind trying to make sense of it all, Nusti had come to the conclusion that he'd tried to push him too hard. The boy had clearly been uncomfortable with getting too close to another faery, and Nusti had gone too far in trying to force a connection with him. It was something he'd never experienced with another faery before; the other gold faeries were more than happy to speak to Nusti whenever he liked, and he enjoyed the camaraderie that came with being part of such a group. He felt included and welcome—not at all a burden.

It hadn't been that way with Crina and, with nobody else to talk to, he was beginning to struggle by himself. His mood was exceptionally low as he made his way aimlessly through the Forest, and it was made worse by the lack of anything meaningful to do. He'd managed to find plenty of the usual berries to sustain himself, but normally, when he was awake, he'd have been busy taking care of the animals of the Forest. Without such commitments to occupy his mind, Nusti was finding it difficult to keep his spirits high.

It was late one morning when Nusti stumbled into a clearing and found himself face to face with a large stag. It had a dark grey coat with occasional white patches, and a strip of deep blue fur ran down its back. Being early Winter, its antlers hadn't yet been cast and crowned the stag's head in their utmost glory, brilliant white and shimmering in the morning sun. The tips of the antlers had taken on a crystalline appearance, and the light shone through them, splitting into a thousand different colours that danced across Nusti's face. The stag stared at him with cold, black eyes, making no noise and standing perfectly still. Nusti stared back, mesmerised by the sight. He'd seen plenty of deer before, but never this close and never in Winter. Besides, there was something different about this one, something that drew him in and, as he approached, he forgot his fear of the unknown for just a moment.

The stag suddenly charged.

The speed with which it leapt towards Nusti took him completely by surprise, though his instincts took over almost immediately. The world seemed to move in slow motion as he crouched ever so slightly and kicked off from the floor, pushing away from the ground with a beat of his wings. He was quick, but barely managed to get out of the way in time as the stag came barrelling past him, snorting in blind rage with its antlers lowered. It charged straight through his Nascent, which briefly exploded into a cloud of leaves before reforming its usual ball shape and following Nusti into the air.

Nusti's speed was his undoing, however, as he hadn't noticed how close he was to the tree he'd been stood underneath. As he shot up and backwards, he collided with the trunk of the tree, badly hurting his arm and crashing down onto a high branch. Barely managing to hold on with his good arm, he panted heavily as he heaved himself onto the branch and out of reach of the stag, which shook its head and huffed before trotting off into the forest.

Leaning back against the trunk, Nusti grasped his injured arm and winced. He wasn't sure if it was broken, but the pain was severe. Ordinarily he'd return to the sleeping chamber to seek out one of the healers, but that wasn't an option right now. Cold, injured and alone, he had no idea what to do, or where to go. He briefly considered seeking out the other snow faeries and asking for help, but his experience with Crina suggested they might act the same towards him. He had nobody but his Nascent, and it couldn't even communicate with him. He considered trying to ask it to go for help, but he didn't know if it would even understand the concept he wanted to convey.

As the sound of the stag moving away through the undergrowth faded to silence, Nusti curled up on the frozen branch and sobbed helplessly, his tears falling to the snow-covered ground below.

IN HIS WINTER

Iphaiut

CHAPTER SEVEN
Reunited

THE STRANGE MAN leant over Nusti as he laid amongst the golden leaves, regarding him with a curious expression. He appeared as a faery, yet he was taller and had no wings upon his back. Nusti's memory stirred, and he recalled stories the elders told of those who came before the Thalim ohr Tainar, *the War for Heaven*. This man was the very image of an aelf, one of the elder races. His eyes, whilst kind, burned with a strange fire that Nusti found he could not describe.

'You are a child out of place, young Nusti,' the strange aelf said. His voice was light and seemed to dance on the air, yet it carried a tone of incredible power. 'You should be asleep like your brothers and sisters.'

'Am I not?' Nusti replied weakly. 'Is this not a dream?' His own voice sounded distant, as though he were hearing himself from afar.

'I mean in the waking world, child,' the aelf replied. 'You must return to the slumber with your brethren.'

'I desire to, but I know not how.' Nusti paused, wishing to speak truthfully. He found his own speech antiquated, though he did not understand why. 'And...and I am fearful of the world in Winter, for all the Forest seems so strange to me. There is a darkness here, in this season, that I have not felt before.'

'And the world will grow darker still, young faery. For terrible things are coming, and you must be ready to face them.'

'How? What things?' Nusti pleaded.

'All in time,' the stranger replied, tugging gently at Nusti's arm. 'You must sleep, but to do so you must first wake up.'

'I do not understand,' Nusti replied. 'Wake to sleep?'

'Wake up, Nusti.' The aelf shook him a little harder.

'Tell me what you mean, I beg of you!'

'Wake up!' Harder still.

'How!?'

'WAKE UP!'

* * *

'WAKE UP, NUSTI!' Crina's voice rang through his ears as Nusti jolted into consciousness, forgetting he was on the tree branch as he flailed about in panic. He would have fallen off the branch entirely were it not for Crina holding him steady by his wounded arm, and he looked in the other boy's eyes in shock.

'Crina? W-what are you doing here?' Nusti asked, his voice trembling slightly as he clutched at Crina's shoulder to keep himself balanced.

'Trying to tend to your arm,' Crina replied, 'which I can't do if you keep moving. Hold still.'

'How did you find me?' Nusti realised he was breathing heavily, and focused in an attempt to try and slow down his breaths.

Crina sighed, pausing briefly as he rolled his eyes. 'The deer are my responsibility, remember?' he replied before continuing to apply a salve to Nusti's bare arm. His touch was exceptionally gentle, and despite the chill of the Winter weather Nusti felt comforted by it. 'I discovered one running through the Forest in fear and, though I couldn't stop it, I managed to follow its tracks back here to try and find out what had spooked it. I have to say, I was surprised to find you here, injured and unconscious.'

'I was asleep?' Nusti asked with a frown. 'But we don't rest outside of the Great Sleep—no faery has ever been able to fall asleep before the end of their season. Though I suppose I'm awake outside of mine, so anything's possible. It's all so messed up.'

Crina said nothing, continuing his work. Nusti's Nascent floated next to the snow faery, observing him curiously as he gently rubbed the salve into the bare skin of Nusti's injured arm. The other boy glanced at it once or twice, though he didn't seem to be bothered by its presence.

'I thought you were gone for good,' Nusti said quietly. He wanted to say more but was afraid of overwhelming Crina with his emotions again.

'So did I,' Crina replied. 'I hadn't intended to come back, but the stag...' He sighed. 'I'm sorry,' he said suddenly.

Nusti blinked; he hadn't expected an apology from the white-haired faery. 'You're sorry? Why?'

'I snapped at you,' Crina replied. 'You were just trying to be friendly, and I pushed you away.' He finished applying the salve and pulled a strip of cloth from a pouch on his waist before carefully wrapping it around Nusti's arm like a bandage. Adjusting himself on the branch so he could lean against the trunk with one leg hanging down, he looked up at the sky through the break in the tree canopy. 'I'm not really used to being with other people,' he said softly, 'even my own kind. They mostly leave me to my own devices, so long as I fulfil my duties when I'm awake.'

Nusti watched Crina as he spoke, searching for some trace of feeling behind his words. Had they been his own, he would have felt pained to speak them, but there was no sadness in Crina's eyes. He spoke as though these were simple facts, with no hint of emotion tied to them.

'Do you...do you mind if I ask why?' Nusti probed tentatively. 'Why do you spend so much time alone, Crina?'

Crina winced slightly at the use of his name, but it was only for a moment. 'I just prefer it,' he replied softly. 'If I'm alone, I don't have to think about what other people are saying or doing, nor do I have to worry about what they expect of me. I can do things the way I want, when I want. At least that way I know what will happen. It's been the same every year, and I'm content with it being that way.'

'Until you met me,' Nusti whispered, realisation dawning on him. Although he felt sad that Crina didn't seem to have bonded with his people, he was also struck by a profound sense of guilt at how he'd disrupted Crina's little bubble. 'I'm sorry,' he sniffed. 'I didn't understand why I seemed to upset you so much until now.'

Crina shook his head. 'It's alright,' he said, swinging his legs round so he was perched on the branch like Nusti. 'It's not that you upset me—you're just...new. Besides, I need to figure out what happened to the stag that attacked you. Come on, I'll help you down to the ground.' He carefully placed his arm around Nusti, and the two boys slowly fluttered down to the Forest floor with Nusti's Nascent following them at a distance.

'Are they usually so aggressive in Winter?' Nusti asked once they'd landed. 'The deer, I mean.'

Crina shook his head again. 'No, and I don't know what's set this one off. The males can be territorial, but they never attack without warning.' He began to step off towards a path through the trees but stopped and turned back to look at Nusti. 'Don't worry,' he said, 'I don't think it was your fault, but we need to find it before it puts others at risk, be it faery or animal.'

Nusti froze at the prospect of encountering his assailant once again, but Crina turned back and held out his hand. 'It'll be alright, I promise,' he said. He didn't smile, but Nusti could have sworn his voice was a little warmer. He took the other boy's hand and allowed him to lead him down the wooded path, feeling significantly less despondent than he had done when Crina had found him. A question still lingered in his mind, however, one that haunted him slightly as the two boys trudged through the trees: what had his dream been about, and why had he slept during his waking days?

IN HIS WINTER

Kihr u am Isil

CHAPTER EIGHT
Death in the Forest

THE BOYS SPENT hours searching the Forest for the deer, carefully scouring the area that Crina had identified as its territory. For the most part, the snow made the deer's movements easy to track; its hoofprints could be seen as depressions in the white blanket covering the Forest floor, but there were places where the snow thinned under the heavier canopies and made the prints difficult to spot. Whilst Nusti struggled to place the tracks, Crina demonstrated an incredible ability to identify disturbances in the brush and foliage, and they would never stop for more than a few moments before moving off in whatever direction he led them. Seemingly eager to join the hunt, Nusti's Nascent would occasionally zoom off ahead to investigate something, before realising it was leaving them behind and hastily returning to Nusti's side.

As they pursued the deer through the Forest, Nusti found himself distracted by many of the differences in the environment. Not all the trees had lost their leaves, and those that remained were covered with a beautiful frost. Icy streams reflected the sunlight, casting strange reflections on the forest around them, and vibrant blue flowers grew on the riverbanks, shaped like little bells that swayed silently in the breeze.

'It's beautiful,' Nusti said quietly as they passed through a dense cluster of trees, causing Crina to look behind him quizzically.

'What is?' he asked, turning back almost immediately to face the path ahead, his attention returning to their search for the deer.

'The Forest,' Nusti replied. 'The colours, the sounds, the feel of it. In Autumn, everything is...well, it's all ending. Even though it's part of the cycle of life in the Forest, there's a feeling of death to it. Most of the animals are preparing to sleep, most of the trees and plants lose their leaves, and the vibrancy of Summer feels a long time past. Winter is like nothing I imagined; it's like time stands still.'

'I suppose,' Crina said with a shrug. 'It's all I've ever known, so I don't know any different.'

'Neither did I until a few days ago,' Nusti mused.

Crina remained silent, continuing his efforts to track

their quarry.

'Wouldn't you like to see the Forest in another season?' Nusti asked.

'I don't know,' Crina replied. 'It's not possible, so I never really thought about it.'

Nusti chuckled. 'I'm here, aren't I?'

'You're an anomaly,' Crina replied bluntly, before stopping so suddenly that Nusti nearly walked into him. 'I'm sorry,' he continued, his voice a touch softer than before. 'I...I didn't mean for that to sound so cold.'

Nusti stepped up next to him and cautiously laid his hand on Crina's shoulder. 'I know,' he said with the slightest of smiles, taking great care not to make the other boy uncomfortable again. Crina didn't pull away, but turned his head to look at Nusti, regarding him with those azure eyes for a time.

'You...you're different from the others,' he said eventually, not looking away.

'What others?' Nusti asked. 'You mean the other snow faeries?'

Crina nodded slowly. 'They don't try to understand me like you do. They just tell me I should be more like them, and that my behaviour is...unnatural.'

'I think you should be whoever or whatever you want to be,' Nusti replied. 'I know the elders tell us we're here to take care of the Forest, but there has to be more to our existence, doesn't there?'

'Maybe,' Crina said quietly. He was silent for a few moments, then nodded to a clearing through the trees. 'Something's moving through there. Come on!' He darted off ahead without warning, leaving Nusti behind him to try and catch up.

As the two boys came to the edge of the clearing, they stopped suddenly. The deer was laid still on the ground, its empty, lifeless eyes a sign to the boys that it was dead, though they were more surprised by the hooded figure that was crouched over it.

'Who is that?' Nusti whispered.

'I don't know,' Crina replied, 'but I'm going to find out.' Before Nusti could stop him, Crina strode out from the treeline and stood before the stranger. His stance was strangely combative, and he folded his arms across his chest as he addressed the interloper. 'Explain yourself,' he said loudly. 'The deer of the Forest are under my protection at this time, and I find you at the body of one I've been tracking. Who are you, and what is your purpose here? Answer me now.'

There was no anger or threat in Crina's voice; just that simple, matter-of-fact tone that he'd gotten so used to. Nusti, whilst wondering if he should step out to help Crina, found himself somewhat in awe of the other boy. As he and his Nascent peered out from behind an ice-covered trunk, he decided to remain hidden and see what happened. Besides, Crina seemed like he could handle himself.

Or at least, he obviously believed he could.

It was at this moment that the stranger chuckled softly in a deep, male voice, and leaning back from the deer he rose to his feet. However, he didn't stop at the usual height of a faery, instead continuing to stand up until he was a good three feet taller than either of the boys. As he did, his hood fell back to reveal long dark hair that was similar in colour to Nusti's, tucked behind pointed ears like his own. The man had no wings, however, and in that moment Nusti realised that this was no faery.

He's an aelf! He looked at the man in shock as something stirred in his memory, tugging at the edge of conscious thought. The man turned to face Crina, and as he did so Nusti caught a glimpse of his eyes. They seemed to burn as though on fire, and in that moment Nusti knew where he recognised the man from. Acting on nothing more than instinct, he stepped out from the treeline and stood next to Crina.

The aelf smiled at him. 'Hello Nusti,' he said warmly. 'It's good to see you in the waking world.'

Nusti felt Crina turn to look at him in shock, and he knew he needed to explain quickly before the other boy drew the wrong conclusion. 'This...aelf, was in my dream,' he said. 'He appeared to me whilst I was sleeping, just before you woke me up. He came as a friend.'

'How...how is that possible?' Crina asked. 'An aelf? They're all supposed to be long dead. And how can you have seen him in your dream? Do you know him?' There was a suspicious look in his eyes, and Nusti realised that the other boy was questioning him.

'No!' he replied quickly, suddenly terrified that Crina's trust in him would evaporate, though he didn't understand why the fear was so strong. 'I've never seen him before that! I don't know what's going on.'

The aelf raised his hands and looked at Crina. 'Please, don't judge your companion harshly,' he urged. 'He speaks the truth; before today he had never laid eyes on me. And whilst we speak of judgement, let me assure you that I am not responsible for this creature's death. I've been tracking it as well, but likely for reasons you may not yet understand.'

Crina's eyes narrowed. 'What do you mean?' he asked.

'What do you feel when you reach out for the Forest around you, Crina?' the aelf asked, gesturing to the trees. How he knew Crina's name was beyond Nusti, but if Crina was unnerved by this, he didn't show it.

'The same as always,' Crina replied. 'I feel the trees, the creatures, the cold of Winter.'

'Go beyond your normal senses, boy,' the aelf said. 'Allow the Forest to connect with you and tell me what you feel.'

Clearly suspicious, Crina remained perfectly still and said nothing as he stared at the elf, apparently refusing to entertain his request. Shaking his head with a grin, the aelf turned to Nusti. 'How about you?' he asked. 'What do you feel?'

Taking a deep breath, Nusti closed his eyes and reached into the Forest around him. He could see the souls of the sleeping creatures burning like gentle candles, and the beating network of roots that criss-crossed through the earth underneath his feet. There was nothing beyond the usual, but he did what the aelf suggested and reached out further with his feelings.

He recoiled in horror as he felt something different, deep beneath the Forest. It was like a writhing, seething mass of pure darkness, unlike anything he'd felt before. It was terribly still, as though lying in wait for something. Terrified that it would notice him, he pulled back immediately as his eyes snapped open.

'What was that!?' he gasped, noticing his Nascent had adopted a form he hadn't seen before. It was pressed flat on his shoulder, laying perfectly still and looking like nothing more than a simple pile of leaves. He frowned but kept his concentration on the aelf.

'What is it?' Crina demanded. 'What did you see?'

'That,' the aelf replied, ignoring Crina as he gestured to the deer's body, 'is what's responsible for the death of this beautiful creature. I don't fully understand it myself, but I do know that whatever sleeps beneath the Forest doesn't belong there.'

'What's beneath the Forest?' Crina demanded. 'And how do you know about all this?' His voice was quiet but had a dangerous edge to it. 'You're not one of us, and the aelves are all gone. Nobody else has the insight you're claiming to possess. Who are you?'

The aelf considered Crina for a moment before replying. 'I'm simply someone who wants to help,' he said softly. 'I concede that you have no reason to trust me, but I assure you that I mean you no harm.'

Ignoring the aelf's plea, Crina turned to Nusti. 'What do you think?' he asked. 'You felt whatever was down there. What do you think we should do?'

Nusti pondered for a moment. 'Whatever it is, it's beyond us,' he admitted. 'We need to seek help from someone higher up.'

'Like one of the elders?' Crina asked.

'Or higher.' Nusti looked at him meaningfully. 'There's one faery who knows this Forest better than anyone.'

Crina paused, eyes widening as he realised the meaning of Nusti's words. 'No, no, absolutely not,' he said, shaking his head. 'There's no way that would be allowed.'

'Crina...she would know. She's connected to the Forest in a way the rest of us aren't, and she might know why I've woken up in Winter too.' Nusti looked at Crina pleadingly. 'It's worth a try.'

'I can't,' Crina whispered. 'I just can't.'

'Why not?' Nusti asked. 'Why are you so afraid of breaking the rules, Crina?'

'I...I can't explain it.' Crina's head dropped, and he looked at the floor dejectedly.

Nusti looked at the white-haired fairy. For whatever reason, Crina was terrified of doing anything that might be considered a contravention of the laws they lived by. What had caused him to become this way? Where was the usual rebellious streak that most young faeries had? 'I'll go alone,' he said eventually. 'You stay here with the deer and tend to the body. That's your duty, right? I wouldn't want to stand in the way of that.'

Crina shook his head. 'You shouldn't break the rules either, especially when you're not in your own season. You don't know what might happen if somebody catches you.'

'I'm still going,' Nusti said defiantly, ignoring the smile on the strange aelf's face. 'I have to know what's going on here, but I'll be back.'

'No.'

'No?'

'No,' Crina repeated, then sighed. 'Whatever happened to that deer, it's my responsibility to find out the truth. As much as I don't want to break the rules, I don't really have a choice.' He stepped towards the strange aelf. 'Whoever you are, you're coming with us.'

The aelf shook his head. 'I'm afraid not, young faery,' he said. 'To do so would jeopardise your journey to finding the answers you seek. I regret I cannot say more, but this is a truth you must discover for yourself, without me.'

Without another word, a gust of icy leaves and snow appeared as if from nowhere and engulfed the aelf in a swirling, rustling vortex. Nusti's Nascent suddenly flew from his shoulder towards the aelf and the mass of white that was twisting around him. Just as quickly as it appeared, however, it was gone, along with the aelf. The two boys stared at the space where he'd just been, then at each other. Nusti's Nascent was left darting back and forth, seemingly confused by the sudden disappearance of the leaves.

'What is going on?' Crina asked. 'Who is he?'

'I don't know,' Nusti replied. 'But there's only one real chance to find any answers.'

Crina sighed. 'I suppose so. But I still think this is a bad idea.'

'I know,' Nusti replied. 'Let's go.'

As they left the clearing and made for the centre of the Forest, Nusti looked back at the spot where the aelf had stood. Who was this stranger, and why had he appeared in his dream mere hours before they'd encountered him in the waking world? He had a feeling the answer was going to be even more complicated than either he or Crina could possibly imagine.

IN HIS WINTER

Amer Vanis Pruhl

CHAPTER NINE
That Joyous Hour

NUSTI AND CRINA trekked with determination through the Forest, heading for its centre where the *Saval'isi*, the Thronetree, stood proud and tall. Towering over the canopies below, it could be seen from the farthest edges of the Forest, the sunlight occasionally breaking through its clustered branches. No other tree could come close to matching its height, as though the Thronetree demanded subservience from all around it.

As he wondered what the Forest must look like from atop the Thronetree, Nusti glanced over at Crina. The other boy was walking beside him with a look of indifference on his face, though Nusti suspected he was simply masking his true feelings about their current destination. Neither of them would normally have any reason, or indeed privilege, to visit the Forest's heart. What must Crina think of the situation Nusti had gotten him into? He felt the guilt again, the feeling that he'd disrupted Crina's world, though the snow faery was showing fewer and fewer signs of being bothered by that.

'The aelf...' Crina said suddenly, interrupting Nusti's train of thought. 'Where do you suppose he came from?'

'I don't know,' Nusti replied. 'Like you said before, they're all supposed to have been wiped out in the War for Heaven. I certainly haven't heard of any aelves being sighted inside the Forest since the first faeries came here.'

'It's not impossible,' Crina said. 'The War for Heaven was supposed to have spanned the known world; there's a chance some escaped the devastation and managed to rebuild.'

Nusti frowned. 'But if that's true, and some did survive, why would one be here?' He mused upon the question for a moment, though Crina's response came quickly.

'We may never know,' the other boy replied. 'Unless we find him again and convince him to tell us what he knows, we've no way of finding out what really happened beyond the Forest Walls. Nobody can fly that high, and the mountains are too steep to try and scale.' Crina paused for a moment, a look of sadness flickering briefly across his face. 'The Forest is a prison as much as it's our home.'

Nusti stared at him in shock. For a faery to speak of

the Forest in such a way was unheard of, even taboo. It was supposed to be a haven for them, a paradise in an otherwise barren world. Did Crina really believe they were prisoners here? 'That's a dark thing to say, Crina,' he whispered.

'Maybe,' Crina replied. 'Doesn't make it any less true though.'

'What do you think she'll make of the aelf?' Nusti asked, trying to change the subject.

'Hard to say,' Crina replied with a shrug. 'Having never met our Beloved Mother, I can't say what kind of a person she is or how she would react to the news of an aelf, a being whose people are supposedly extinct, wandering around inside the Forest. She's the only one left with any memory of them, so arguably she would know straight away if she saw him whether he's one of the old ones or not.'

Nusti nodded as they continued towards the Thronetree. The Forest was changing slightly as they drew closer to its centre. The trees here were taller, and their trunks broader. The woods seemed more 'organised'; the placement of trees and bushes was less random, as though the centre of the Forest had been cultivated to a particular design. His Nascent's behaviour also became less erratic; it moved along a smooth, deliberate line, as though following an unseen path that permeated the air itself.

Nusti's attention was suddenly drawn to a large clearing visible through the trees. Heading towards it, he realised it was a large pond where he'd spent many autumnal evenings in the past. Being Winter, however, it was now a solid, glassy floor of ice. It was the first time Nusti had seen frozen water, and he marvelled at how breathtaking it looked with the sunlight reflecting off its surface.

'This is your first time seeing ice, right?' Crina asked from behind him.

Nusti nodded. 'It's wonderful,' he whispered.

'You can step on it if you like,' Crina said as he strode onto the surface of the pond. He held out his hand towards Nusti. 'Come here.' Nusti stepped onto the edge of the ice, taking great care not to slip. 'Don't worry, you won't fall through,' Crina assured him.

'Wait, what?' Nusti asked with wide eyes. 'What do you mean fall through?'

Crina gave him a puzzled look. 'You know it's only the top that's frozen, right?' he asked. 'There's still water underneath the surface.' Nusti looked around him in a slight panic and, in that moment, Crina visibly suppressed a smile. 'You're not heavy enough to break the ice layer,' he said warmly. 'It's perfect for a little dance.'

A *dance*? Nusti stared at him, wondering how someone could possibly dance on such a slippery surface. Not only that, but the notion of Crina dancing seemed a little hard to believe. As he watched, however, the other boy stepped away and lifted one of his legs slightly. Holding his hand over the sole of his foot, he gestured slightly with his fingers and icy blue wisps issued forth from his fingertips. *That's ice magic*, Nusti realised. They coalesced in a line down the sole of his boot, forming what looked like a blade of ice. Placing his foot down and repeating the act with the other, Crina was now balanced on the two icy blades. He stood a little taller than Nusti now, and with his confident demeanour on the ice he appeared the most comfortable he'd been since they'd met.

'You can use ice magic!' Nusti exclaimed. 'That must be so much fun!'

'It has its uses,' Crina replied. 'You'd be surprised how versatile it can be.' He traced lines in the ice with the blades on his feet, moving them back and forth one after the other.

'What are those for?' Nusti asked, puzzled.

'This,' Crina replied, and with no warning he took off across the ice, pushing off with one leg and then the other. The blades allowed him to glide across the surface of the frozen pond, each leaving a thin score in the ice as he passed. His movement was incredibly graceful, as though he were born for nothing less than dancing across the ice. Nusti stared in awe as Crina navigated the pond, turning in large circles and then small ones. It looked difficult, but Nusti was content just to watch Crina enjoying himself. And he was; the boy visibly relaxed into his movements, as though he didn't have a care in the world.

Then he started doing it backwards.

Somehow, Crina managed to turn on the spot and adjust his stance, so he was pushing away from the ice in a different way. He made his way around the edge of the pond with his back to his direction of travel the whole time, until eventually he arrived back where Nusti was stood. He spun around with a leg out wide, coming to a stop with a small spray of frosty ice. Nusti was speechless, and Crina let slip another smile before he could stop himself.

'Would you like to try?' he asked, cocking his head slightly.

Nusti shook his head. 'How do you do that? I wouldn't be able to stand up, let alone do what you do.'

'It's easier than you think,' Crina replied. 'Come on, put your hand on my shoulder and lift up your leg with the other one.'

Nusti did as he was asked, and watched as Crina summoned a blade of ice like his onto the sole of Nusti's left boot. Despite Nusti's Nascent trying its hardest to get in the way, likely out of curiosity, Crina managed to successfully affix the ice to Nusti's boot. 'Now the other one,' he said, repeating the process on Nusti's right boot. His feet felt heavier, and he grasped Crina's shoulder as he struggled to maintain his balance.

'This is strange,' Nusti said. 'I'm not sure I like it.'

'You'll be fine once you're on the move,' Crina said, taking Nusti's hand in his and beginning to pull him along. It wasn't a comfortable sensation, and Nusti wobbled significantly for a few minutes as he tried to get his balance. Crina guided him in how to move his feet, and after a while he encouraged Nusti to try for himself. 'Off you go!' he said as he gave Nusti a little push.

For his part, Nusti managed to glide quite smoothly for several seconds, accompanied by his Nascent which floated just above the surface of the ice, apparently observing how his feet were moving. Unfortunately, his balance wasn't yet perfect, and he began to wobble again. 'Move your feet!' Crina called out from behind him, but it was too late. The wobble turned into a fall, and before he knew it Nusti's feet had disappeared from under him, and he fell squarely on his rear onto the hard ice. He winced in pain for a moment, but was soon distracted by a new, wonderful noise.

Crina was laughing.

It was a sound of pure joy, an emotion that Nusti hadn't seen from Crina thus far. The boy was clutching his stomach as he giggled uncontrollably at the sight of Nusti sat on the ice rubbing his behind. His voice was rich, and for the first time since they met Nusti felt like he was seeing Crina's true self, the one he hid behind his usual cold mask. It was wonderful to watch, and it brought a single happy tear to Nusti's eyes.

As though realising that he'd let said mask slip, Crina stopped laughing abruptly. He looked at Nusti with discomfort visible on his face, before gliding over and helping him to his feet. 'We should probably move on,' he said. 'It'll be dark soon and we need to make our way closer to the Thronetree before we lose the light.'

Despite his frustration at Crina's insistence on withdrawing back into his shell, Nusti nodded silently and allowed the other boy to remove the blades from his feet and drop them to the ice where they fragmented into dust. His Nascent briefly examined the patch where the icy blades had disintegrated, then slowly rose to settle by Nusti's shoulder, as though it were dejected at the loss of the magical skates. As they left the pond and headed back into the trees, Nusti pushed down the feeling of frustration and allowed himself some small comfort in one thing.

He'd made Crina laugh.

IN HIS WINTER

1 Sil o a Hasha

CHAPTER TEN
A Leaf out of Season

SEEING THE THRONETREE up close was an otherworldly experience, Nusti decided as the two boys approached the base of the trunk the following morning. The tops of the roots were as thick as a normal tree trunk and dug deep into the earth, spreading outwards from the base and splitting the ground apart. Snow blanketed them, and the same blue winter flowers that Nusti had seen earlier grew in the crevices between them.

Something was amiss, however. Whilst he didn't know much about Winter, Nusti could feel that things weren't as they should be. There was a noticeable absence of life in the vicinity of the Thronetree; for a location that was supposed to be the beating heart of the Forest, there wasn't so much as a scampering rodent or chittering bird in sight. As he looked up at the Thronetree, he saw the occasional leaf falling slowly to the ground. *This is wrong,* he thought. *The Thronetree doesn't lose its leaves.* As one landed in front of him, he picked it up and examined it with a frown. It was a pure white leaf unlike anything he'd seen before. 'Is this... normal?' he asked Crina. 'White leaves?'

Crina nodded and picked up another leaf, tenderly stroking its edges. 'The leaves turn white in winter to mark the season; I assume it's the same for the other seasons.'

Nusti shook his head. 'They're gold in Autumn, but so are all the other trees. None of the other trees in the Forest have leaves like this in Winter.'

'It's the Thronetree,' Crina replied with a shrug. 'The magic imbued within it must do lots of strange things that don't happen in the rest of the Forest.' Nusti's Nascent suddenly appeared from over Crina's shoulder and wove itself around the hand that was holding the leaf, causing the boy to recoil. 'Get off!' he hissed, dropping the leaf and waving the Nascent away. 'Can't you control it?' he asked, looking at Nusti expectantly.

'Not really,' Nusti replied. 'They bond with us, and follow us, but really they just do what they want.' He paused. Was now the time to ask about Crina's Nascent?

It had to be. He didn't know what to expect once they ascended the Thronetree. Anything could happen up there, and he might lose the opportunity to ask the question

IN HIS WINTER

forever. 'Crina?' he said softly. 'I want to know about your Nascent.'

Crina closed his eyes but didn't clench his fists like the last time Nusti had tried to ask. 'Why do you want to know?' he asked, turning to look at Nusti. 'Why does it matter to you?'

Nusti took a breath. 'I think partly because it's unusual, but also because I want to understand you more. I can't imagine life without my Nascent—I'd like to hear what it's like for you.'

Silence fell over the pair for a moment, broken only by the rustling of Nusti's Nascent which was playing with a leaf that had fallen from the Thronetree, seeing how long it could keep it from landing on the ground. Crina looked at it, and Nusti saw a great sadness in his eyes.

'Do you remember your nascence, Nusti?' Crina asked.

Nusti pulled a face. 'Bits and pieces. Mostly flashes of experience, moments of pure curiosity, the same as most faeries. Mostly I remember just acting on instinct.' He paused. 'What about you?'

Crina shuffled his feet. 'I don't remember any of mine,' he said softly. 'I must have been a Nascent, otherwise I wouldn't be here now, but I didn't retain any of the memories or experiences when I was reborn.'

Nusti's jaw dropped. 'None of it?' he asked. 'How did you...I mean, what happened? You'd have had to learn everything from scratch.'

Crina nodded slightly. 'It started when no Nascent came to bond with me. At first the others thought it was something wrong with the Nascents, that maybe they didn't recognise me as a newborn. But eventually they realised that I was the problem. I couldn't act on my own, I could barely communicate with anyone. The elders, they... they, um...' He trailed off, and Nusti realised there were tears forming in Crina's eyes. *He's actually crying,* Nusti thought. He wanted to reach out and hug Crina, but his experience of the last few days told him to simply let the boy work through it in his own way. Crina wiped his eyes on his sleeve and sniffed slightly. 'The elders met to decide what was to be done with me,' he continued. 'There was lots of discussion, but in the end the majority agreed that the burden of teaching me from the beginning was too great, and it would be better for the Forest if they simply tried again with another reborn faery.'

Nusti frowned. 'That doesn't make sense,' he said. 'The only way they could do that is...if...' He gasped as he realised the gravity of what Crina was saying, and held his hands over his mouth in shock. The other boy looked at him, tears still in his eyes, and nodded.

'They wanted to kill me, Nusti,' he whispered, his voice breaking slightly. 'They were actually going to kill a newborn because I was deemed to be too great a burden. They would have done it too, but they needed a unanimous decision.'

'What happened?' Nusti asked, his own voice breaking as he tried not to join Crina in tears.

'The elder that oversaw my cot spoke for me. Maybe he felt protective, or maybe he didn't like the idea of a child being killed; I'm not sure. Regardless, he refused to agree with the other elders, and so they were forced to let me live. In return, he was the one ordered to teach me how to be a faery.

'At first, he seemed to relish the task. He enjoyed teaching me, and it seemed like a novelty to him. But when I began to struggle with some concepts, or I couldn't understand why I had to interact with other faeries, he became increasingly frustrated. It wasn't long before he left me to my own devices and, once I knew enough to survive on my own, I stopped looking for help.'

Nusti stared at him, blinking away tears from his eyes. Crina had stopped crying, but the truth behind the pain in his eyes was clear: he'd only ever had one person to support him, and that man had eventually abandoned him for the very reason his elders had wanted to extinguish his life in the first place.

'I'm so sorry, Crina,' Nusti whispered. 'I can't imagine what it must have been like for you.'

Crina shrugged. 'I'm alive, and I haven't needed anyone's help since he washed his hands of me. I'm fine.'

'Yes, but...' Nusti trailed off as he noticed something odd about the leaf he was holding. Amber colour was bleeding into the otherwise pure white at the tips of the leaf, like ink spreading across parchment.

Like...like the colour of leaves in Autumn.

Crina stepped over to join him and, as the boys watched, the white of the leaf slowly withdrew, leaving it a crisp amber colour. It was as though time had reversed, undoing the change of Winter. It was strange to watch, and Nusti looked up at Crina to see what he made of it.

The boy's eyes were wide, staring at him with a mixture of apprehension and fear. 'What is it?' Nusti asked, ignoring his Nascent which was presently floating next to his hand, brushing itself against the leaf ever so slightly.

'You...you turned the leaf back,' Crina replied, stumbling back slightly. 'Back to its Autumn self.'

'No, I didn't!' Nusti shook his head. 'It wasn't me!'

'I saw you, Nusti!' Crina exclaimed. 'You picked it up and it changed back. You're...*you're undoing Winter.*' He half-hissed, half-whispered the last part, as though even speaking of it would draw unwanted attention.

'How? I didn't even know I was doing it...' Nusti's bottom lip began to tremble as Crina's accusatory tone stabbed at his heart. The other boy noticed his wavering voice and sighed, stepping closer and fixing Nusti with a pointed look.

'I didn't mean to accuse you of intent,' Crina said, 'but we need to stop this, Nusti, before the Custodian realises what's going on. I don't know much about her, but my guess is she wouldn't be too happy about the natural cycle of seasons being thrown off. She might even send her guardians to deal with you.'

As if on cue, the ground around them erupted. Four pulsating mounds of dark, moist earth rose up, throwing snow and soil to the floor, followed by what appeared to be a combination of vines and creaking wood. As the boys cowered before them, the mounds slowly twisted into vaguely humanoid shapes, towering over them as they grew. Eventually they settled, each one staring at them with something akin to a face. Nusti's Nascent retreated behind him, and he could actually feel it pressed flat against his back.

The Avatars of the Forest, Nusti thought. *The protectors of the Custodian.*

The one closest to Nusti spoke, but not with words; he heard the creature's voice in his mind. YOU ARE THE *REN O A HASHA*, it said. THE BOY OUT OF SEASON. YOUR AWAKENING DISTURBS THE FOREST AND DISRUPTS ITS NATURAL ORDER.

'I'm sorry,' Nusti said, his voice trembling with fear. 'I didn't mean for any of this to happen. I don't know why I'm awake.'

IT MATTERS NOT. SHE WILL DECIDE WHAT IS TO BE DONE WITH YOU BOTH.

'Both?' Nusti asked, looking at Crina in confusion. 'What does he have to do with this?'

The Avatar ignored him and gestured to the trunk of the Thronetree, where a winding staircase was forming out of more vines. Come, it said as it moved towards the stair, and as Nusti went to follow it Crina suddenly grabbed his arm.

'Are you sure about this?' he asked, looking uncertain. 'We don't know how she's going to react to you.'

'Do we have a choice?' Nusti replied. 'Besides, you just said we need to stop whatever's happening.'

'I know, but...' Crina looked at the floor. 'Never mind.'

'What?'

'Nothing. Let's just go.'

As the two boys began to climb the winding stair, Nusti couldn't shake the feeling that something terrible was waiting for them at the top. He couldn't quite put his finger on it, but he hoped with all his heart that it wasn't the one they'd travelled all this way to meet.

After all, if the Custodian of the Forest wouldn't help him, where else could he turn?

IN HIS WINTER

Am Umadanul

CHAPTER ELEVEN
The Custodian

THE THRONETREE'S CROWN was practically a palace, and Nusti looked around in awe as he and Crina were led into the open-air chamber at its very centre. Branches and vines formed tall, ornate columns that surrounded them in a ring, and the floor was made of a glassy, petrified wood that was arrayed in complex patterns which couldn't possibly have been achieved naturally. It was breathtaking, but his attention was quickly drawn to the figure waiting for them on the other side of the room.

Paler'an, the First Faery and Custodian of the Forest, fixed Nusti with a cold stare as he and Crina were brought before her. She was radiantly beautiful, with a golden crown resting on long blonde hair that flowed over her shoulders and down to her waist as she sat on her throne of vines and winter flowers. Her delicate robes appeared to be woven from a combination of spider silks and fine cotton, with winter leaves layered over her bodice. The most entrancing thing about her was her wings, which were entirely golden and appeared as though they were made from metal. Altogether, she had an almost ethereal quality, as though she wasn't quite there. Nusti had never dreamed he would meet her, but as he stood wilting under her gaze, in that moment he wished he could be literally anywhere else.

She dismissed the Avatars with a wave of her hand, who collapsed into the floor as though they'd never existed, the pulsating wood and vines of their bodies merging seamlessly with the polished wood of the Thronetree. Nusti's Nascent gusted over to the spot where one of them had disappeared, trying without success to merge into the floor too. Nusti and Crina now stood alone before Paler'an, both boys too terrified to speak. In that moment, her gaze shifted from Nusti to Crina, and the cold look in her eyes was quickly replaced by warmth and kindness. She looked upon Crina as a mother might look at their child, and a gentle smile crept onto her lips.

'Crina, my special one,' she said with a voice like velvet. 'I had wondered when I might find you here in my home.'

'M-me, Beloved Mother?' Crina stuttered slightly, which Nusti found surprising. He'd mostly spoken with confidence around Nusti, but standing in the presence of the Custodian seemed to have robbed him of that bold spirit.

'Of course,' Paler'an replied. 'All my children stand before me at some point in their lives, and I have watched you with interest for some time now. Ever alone, bereft of Nascent, but always focussed on your duties. Despite the difficult start you faced, you have overcome every challenge on your path. Your unwavering dedication to maintaining the order and balance of the Forest is unusual for a juvenile faery, though not unwelcome. You have achieved much despite your youth, Crina, and I am very proud of you.'

Crina's face spasmed slightly, as though he were battling to control his emotions again. He said nothing but bowed his head in respect and gratitude. Nusti remained silent, waiting to see what else she had to say.

'I sense, however, that you are discontented.' Her eyes narrowed slightly, but she continued to wear her smile as she spoke. It gave her an almost sinister look, and Nusti suppressed a shudder. 'Tell me,' she said, still talking to Crina, 'what troubles you, child?'

Crina paused, looking at Nusti as he struggled for an answer. He stuttered briefly, then looked at the floor dejectedly, unable to form the words. Paler'an sighed and turned to Nusti; the warmth she had shown Crina disappeared in an instant. She wore that cold expression once more, and Nusti tried his best to maintain his composure in front of the Custodian even as his Nascent flew back over to float by his shoulder.

'And you,' she said with an icy tone, eyeing the Nascent briefly before turning her gaze on Nusti. 'I would have you would explain what exactly you think you are doing, young Nusti.'

Nusti paused. 'I-I don't understand, Beloved Mother,' he said softly, afraid to anger her.

'Do you not? Awake out of season, interrupting the natural order of things? Even turning the leaves back to their autumnal selves? Such actions are unprecedented and unwelcome, and I have little patience for them. My Forest is ancient, child. I have stood watch over it for ten thousand years, keeping our people safe, caring for them where nobody else would. That is my calling, yet for the first time in memory that duty is under threat, and from one of my own, no less.'

'It's not on purpose,' Nusti began to protest, before Paler'an silenced him with a wave of her hand.

'Your intent is irrelevant, child. You are harming the Forest, and I have sensed the darkness growing as a result. We faeries have lived here in peace and harmony for thousands of years, and not once has that serenity had cause to falter. Tell me: would you be our doom?'

'I don't want to do anything to hurt anyone!' Nusti protested. 'I just want to understand why all this is happening.'

'Lies!' Paler'an cried. 'I have seen your heart, young one.

You seek our undoing!'

Nusti frowned. This was not the Paler'an he'd been told about; the kind and loving protector of the Forest was instead a cold and judgmental woman who refused to listen to reason. How could he convince her that he bore no ill intent?

'I felt it too,' Nusti said suddenly. 'Down in the Forest, I could feel something in the depths, something that doesn't belong there. It felt wrong, and malevolent.' If he could persuade her that the darkness was to blame, and not him, maybe she would back down.

Paler'an, however, looked furious, and Nusti immediately regretted telling her about his encounter. 'You...you're connected to it!' she hissed. 'You're the reason for the Forest's pain, its torment. What are you planning, boy?' She rose from her throne, and the two boys cowered back slightly.

'Nothing!' cried Nusti. 'I don't understand what's happened—that's why I came here seeking your help!'

Paler'an paused, then stepped down from her dais. 'I will do what must be done,' she said quietly. 'I will help you find the sleep you seek.'

'W-what are you going to do?' Nusti asked, trembling in fear. He could feel Crina step towards him, an atmosphere of trepidation surrounding the young snow faery. Nusti's Nascent trembled in the air behind him.

'The balance must be restored,' Paler'an replied. 'You

should be asleep...and sleep you shall.' She raised her hand, and smoke began to emerge from it. Two inky, misty helixes of magical essence wrapped around her arm: one of deepest red, and the other of blue-purple. It was not the magick of the Forest, or any of the other magicks of which Nusti was aware. The elder faery toyed with the smoke, weaving it around her fingers as she continued to stare at him. 'I am sorry to have to do this to you, my child,' she whispered. 'I promise, you will remember nothing of what has happened, and you will awaken at the start of the next Autumn as you should. It will be as though nothing has changed.'

As she raised her hand towards Nusti, strange power coiling around it, he realised what was happening. She intended to put him to sleep with magick, to send him back to the chamber with the rest of his kind. Whilst his head told him this was the right thing to do, his heart pounded in defiance, and he looked over at Crina as a terrifying thought entered his mind.

Was this the last he would see of his new friend?

Uruth a'i Ren

CHAPTER TWELVE
A Boy's Resolve

CRINA'S VOICE RANG out as Nusti was about to close his eyes and surrender himself to Paler'an's magick. 'No, you can't!' He turned his head to see Crina stood ready, with a determined expression on his little face and his feet planted wide in a stance that suggested he was prepared to do something incredibly foolish. Nusti's Nascent breezed over and floated next to Crina, as though showing solidarity with him.

'Crina...what are you doing?' Nusti asked quietly.

'I would ask the same question, child,' Paler'an added, her voice cold once more. Her hand was still raised, magick surging around it. 'Whilst I take no pleasure in doing this, it must be done; surely you understand?'

'I...I don't want him to sleep,' Crina replied. 'I'm...I'm lonely.' The words hit Nusti like a splash of cold water. Crina? Lonely? Was this what the other boy had been battling with?

'I've watched you for a long time, child,' Paler'an said, her eyes studying Crina carefully. 'You've always spent time alone, away from the other snow faeries. You've always been content in yourself; don't let this deviant boy change who you are.' Crina looked at Nusti, and his eyes revealed a deeper truth. He was lonely, and Nusti could feel it, like something pulling at him from within Crina. 'He's not like the others,' Crina continued. 'He's different somehow. I...I want him to stay.'

Nusti blinked away tears as the sincerity of Crina's words sunk in. He'd wondered whether the other boy had heard or felt anything he'd tried to do for him, and a lot of the time it had seemed like he was just an annoyance to him. But here, now, Crina was saying that wanted Nusti to remain with him. It was so gratifying, and Nusti's heart warmed.

'And?' Paler'an's voice was even colder now, with a dangerous edge. 'It changes nothing. This gold faery must sleep, and you must return to your duties.'

Crina shook his head. 'But I don't want that.'

'Enough!' Paler'an snapped. 'What you want is irrelevant! The balance must be restored!' The magick coursing through her hand intensified, and she thrust her arm towards Nusti. He watched as the spell surged forwards, crackling with radiant energy. Part of him wanted to look away, but he found that he couldn't. He could only stare, panicked, as the magick ripped through the air towards him.

He didn't notice that Crina had moved from his side until the other boy was in front of him, arms spread out as though trying to protect him from the magick. Did he intend to take the force of the spell himself, and sleep before he was due? His Nascent hung between the two boys, itself arrayed in a hexagonal pattern almost like a snowflake.

A wall of solid ice suddenly erupted from the wood beneath them, shooting up just inches from Crina's face and forming a solid barrier between them and Paler'an. Her spell hit the wall and dissipated into the air, leaving a strange aura hanging over them. The ice creaked, but remained solid, and for a moment there was no sound atop the Thronetree but a deadly silence that hung over them all.

Paler'an's shriek broke that silence before Nusti could comprehend what had just happened, and fear suddenly gripped him. He looked at Crina, who turned to face him and nodded. Their instincts taking over, the two boys turned and ran for the vine stairs with Nusti's Nascent close behind, desperate to get away from Paler'an and her apparent determination to separate them. Behind them, Nusti heard the sound of ice breaking, and turned back to see the elder faery bursting through Crina's wall of ice as though it were suddenly immaterial. She reached out her hand once more, but the magick was different this time.

Shimmering green vines shot forth from her throne, darting around her and heading straight for Crina. *This was her true power,* Nusti realised. As the boys reached the top of the stairs they'd ascended earlier, one of the vines coiled around Crina's left wing and constricted, crumpling it like paper. He cried out in pain and stumbled, and Nusti stopped to help him. As he reached down to help Crina and saw Paler'an bearing down on them, he realised they would never make it down the stairs. Taking the other boy by the waist and placing his arm around his neck, he threw a hateful glare back at Paler'an, the one who was supposed to be their protector. She had abandoned that role, and as Nusti met her crazed eyes he realised she sought more than his slumber. She meant to do them both harm for defying her, and there would be no reasoning with her. There was only one thing left for them to do, and that was run.

The boys jumped.

IN HIS WINTER

Avil Nim Trahna ti Prinalla

CHAPTER THIRTEEN
We'll Face it Together

THE TWO LITTLE faeries struggled through the Forest, driven forward by the terrifying shrieks echoing through the trees behind them. Paler'an hadn't stopped her pursuit once they'd jumped from the Thronetree, and despite Nusti straining his wings to slow their descent, he wasn't used to the weight of another faery, meaning they'd suffered a rough landing. He'd twisted his ankle slightly, leaving him with a limp that was only getting worse as he tried to run, and his chest was still tight from the cold. Crina's crumpled wing was twitching against his back, and the pain was evident in his face from the way he winced. Between them, they were barely keeping ahead of the vines and thorns that Paler'an was throwing after them. As they fled, Nusti silently wondered how much longer they could carry on for.

'Crina,' he panted as they ducked under a low hanging branch, 'why did you protect me? Why did you put yourself in harm's way just for me?'

The other boy said nothing but made a soft grunt as his damaged wing knocked against a tree trunk. Nusti slowed for him, but Crina shook his head. 'Keep going,' he wheezed, and shoved Nusti forwards. His Nascent darted back and forth between them, apparently having developed some attachment to Crina as well, though it couldn't have been a full bonding.

They continued for some time, pushed ever onwards by the thought of what awaited them should they be caught by Paler'an. It was a strange thing to Nusti; for so many years he'd been told that she protected the Forest and all within it, but she had been frighteningly quick to turn against them when they threatened the status quo. What would the other faeries think of what had happened? Could he ever go back to his people when the very heart of the Forest had turned against him?

'Where do we go?' he asked suddenly. 'There's no way we can hide from her or get far enough away that she'll let us go.'

'I don't know,' Crina replied.

'Could we leave? Over the mountains?' It was madness to suggest it, but Nusti couldn't think of another option that would keep them safe from Paler'an.

Crina stared at him as though he was insane. 'What!? That's foolishness, and you know it. The mountains are too steep to scale, and with my wing I couldn't possibly make it. Besides, there's nothing outside the Forest. We'd be fleeing into a wasteland. I...*we* couldn't survive out there, Nusti. We'd be dead in a matter of days.'

Would we though? Nusti was beginning to question much of what he knew, and he was starting to suspect the outside world may not have been everything they were told. For one thing, where had the aelf come from? Were there more of his kind, survivors like Crina had suggested? And what about what Paler'an had said before: keeping them safe? From what?

'Maybe *I* deserve for her to catch me,' Crina continued, 'but not you.' He sighed. 'You've done nothing wrong, and now because of me she's hunting both of us. I'm sorry.'

'Hey,' Nusti said, pulling Crina to a stop. Though the sounds behind them were getting closer, he didn't care, and he took Crina's hands in his. 'Don't be sorry. You protected me, and I'll never hold that against you. Thank you.' And then, without a moment of hesitation, he threw his arms around Crina and hugged him. Nusti fully expected him to pull away, but to his surprise the other boy didn't. Crina awkwardly kept his arms by his sides, but Nusti felt his cold little chin rest gently on his shoulder. 'Thank you, Nusti,' Crina whispered. 'Thank you for showing me what it means not to be alone.'

'No matter what happens,' Nusti said, 'we can survive so long as we're together. It'll be alright.'

A slight breeze ruffled his hair, and he felt a sudden, yet comforting shiver run up his spine.

'You know, I do believe you're correct, young Nusti.' The familiar voice came from the direction of the outer Forest, and the two boys pulled away from their embrace to see its owner. The dark-haired aelf stood before them once more, smiling broadly.

'Now, what exactly is it you two have gotten yourselves into?'

Am Nurim

CHAPTER FOURTEEN
The Hunter

NUSTI STARED APPREHENSIVELY at the aelf; whilst he was certainly surprised at his appearance, he was also somewhat suspicious that they should just *happen* to run into him as they were fleeing from Paler'an. The chances of encountering him at this particular moment were slim, and he had a strong feeling that the aelf had been watching them for a long time now.

'What are you doing here?' Crina asked, as though reading Nusti's mind. He was still wincing from the pain his broken wing was causing him, and the words came between agonised gasps.

'I just happened to be out for a quiet stroll in the Forest,' the aelf replied. 'What about you two? You look like you're in something of a hurry.'

Crina remained silent, but Nusti threw a glance over his shoulder. 'We're being chased,' he replied.

'By whom?'

'...I don't want to say.' Nusti knew they needed help, but he still didn't quite trust the strange aelf who had thus far kept his identity a secret from them.

'It seems strange for two young faeries to be running *away* from the direction of the Thronetree,' the aelf replied. 'Why don't you tell me what's going on? Maybe I can help.'

'Nusti, we can't trust him,' Crina hissed. 'He might be one of hers.'

'Hers?' the aelf asked, before a look of realisation crept onto his face. 'Ahhh, I see. You're running from the Custodian.'

Nusti paused, then nodded nervously. Crina remained perfectly still, but his eyes flashed in defiance. 'What's it to you?' he asked.

'I see two young faeries in distress,' the aelf replied, 'yet the Forest is supposed to be a place of peace. Why is it, then, that Paler'an is pursuing her own children?'

The two boys exchanged a look, before Nusti turned back to the aelf. 'She tried to put me back to sleep,' he replied nervously.

'Because you're awake out of season.' The aelf frowned. 'You slept right through Autumn and awoke in Winter.'

'You know?'

IN HIS WINTER

'It's fairly obvious, Nusti,' the aelf chuckled. 'I know enough about the Forest to know that only the snow faeries should be awake at this time. For some reason, you woke up late.'

Nusti nodded. 'I know. What I don't know is why.'

'What *I'd* like to know is why you've seen fit to defy her will,' the aelf said quietly. 'Returning you to the Great Sleep may restore the cycle of the Forest; surely you can see that she's only doing what she believes is best?'

'I-I was ready to sleep,' Nusti whispered. 'I didn't want to cause any more trouble, but...' He looked at Crina, unsure how to continue.

'But I stopped her,' Crina interjected. 'I...couldn't let her take Nusti away from me.'

Nusti looked at him, that warm feeling creeping back into his heart.

'And why not?' the aelf asked softly, raising an eyebrow quizzically.

To Nusti's surprise, Crina looked at him for a moment before taking his hand and squeezing it ever so slightly. 'Because he's my friend,' the little faery replied, 'and I don't want to be without a friend ever again.'

Nusti found himself unable to say anything. His heart was pounding in his chest, though whether it was from fear of their pursuer or joy at Crina's words, he couldn't say. All he knew was that he didn't want to be parted from the other boy either.

The aelf smiled at them both. 'That is as noble a reason as any, but I fear it has put you both at risk. I must ask: what will you do now?'

Nusti, busy trying to fight back tears, shook his head. 'I don't know,' he whispered. 'Can you help us?'

The aelf frowned, then his eyes widened slightly. 'I may be able to, but we have to deal with something first.'

'What do you mean?' Crina asked.

The aelf nodded behind them. 'That,' he said grimly, causing the two boys to turn around. The Forest crashed apart behind them and Paler'an emerged into the clearing, borne forth on an impressive but terrifying flurry of vines and leaves. Her face was one of pure rage, but when she saw the aelf her expression turned to icy shock.

'Aelf!' she hissed. 'What are you doing in *my* Forest?' Her voice was shaky, and Nusti could see she was physically shaking in anger. She didn't seem shocked at his existence however, and a suspicion began to grow in his mind.

'Simply taking a stroll,' the aelf replied plainly, and Nusti almost smiled as he remembered that had been his coy answer to them not a few moments earlier.

'You do not belong here!' Paler'an snapped. 'Your kind are forbidden to enter my Forest!'

The full meaning of her words hit Nusti like a rock. *Your* kind. There were more aelves, others like the one before them, and Paler'an knew about them. There was life beyond the Forest, and that meant she'd lied to them. To all the faeries.

'Why are you pursuing these two boys?' the aelf said, ignoring her previous words. 'They seem quite frightened to me.'

'Do not presume to interfere in the affairs of the Forest,' Paler'an snarled. 'You have no say in what happens here. Return to your own lands and leave this matter to me.'

The aelf didn't move. 'I'm afraid I can't do that,' he said. 'You see, they've told me a rather distressing tale, one in which you're trying to do harm to them.'

Paler'an snorted. 'Nonsense,' she declared. 'I seek only to return this one to sleep, as he should be.' Her gaze fell upon Nusti, who fought against his instinct to cower before her.

'And you believe that will fix what's wrong with our Forest?' the aelf asked. 'How are you so sure that Nusti is the cause, and not merely a symptom? And what of the effect on young Crina? Look at how he's grown from what he used to be thanks to his newfound friendship with Nusti. Would you break his spirit by tearing that away from him?'

Nusti frowned. What did he mean by *our* Forest?

'Do not speak to me as though you know anything of me or my people,' Paler'an replied. 'These are my children, and I have watched over them and all who preceded them since we first came into existence. I will not defer to a *siraelf* in these matters; the Forest is *mine*, and I will decide how best to protect it.'

The wind blew softly through the clearing as her final

words hung in the air, and Nusti realised she'd used a term from many millennia ago. She'd referred to the man as a wood aelf, one of the old races believed lost. That now seemed to be a lie, one Paler'an had maintained despite knowledge of people outside the Forest. Unsure what to do, the boys waited nervously for whatever would come next.

The aelf, however, simply sighed, shaking his head as he stepped towards her. 'After all this time, nothing has changed. I'm so disappointed in you, *avi imthet*.' His final words were spoken in a lower register, as though his voice had completely changed, and Nusti knew what they meant.

Avi imthet. My daughter.

Paler'an's gasp was audible, and the two boys looked at her. 'You...it can't be,' she whispered, tears suddenly forming in her eyes. 'Not here, not now.' Her voice trembled, and Nusti looked from her to the aelf, entirely unprepared for what happened next.

He shimmered.

Light briefly shone through the aelf, as though he wasn't really there. Half a second later he became solid again, then shimmered once more. As the boys watched, his form began to change and shift. Tendrils of green magic wove around him, and his clothing changed from dark leathers to a strange mixture of cloth and leaf. His hair lightened slightly to a rich auburn colour, and a crown of antlers coalesced around his head as his eyes turned brilliant green, seeming to glow with an otherworldly light. His entire presence had changed, and he now appeared taller, stronger and immensely powerful.

'Nusti,' Crina whispered. 'He's...he's...'

Nusti said nothing; he could only stare open-mouthed as he realised who the man, stood before them in divine glory, really was. He was no mere aelf. He was The Hunter, Lord of Forests, Father of all Faeries.

He was Nurim'isil. Their god.

1 Alais Aisharut

CHAPTER FIFTEEN
A God Revealed

THE THREE FAERIES stood in utter silence as they gazed upon the awesome vision of their god stood before them, glowing radiantly as he regarded them with a peaceful look upon his face. Nusti's Nascent slowly turned in the air, its cloud of dispersed leaves hanging perfectly still, as though it were suspended in time. Paler'an had lost any semblance of her wrathful countenance; she simply stood behind the two boys, whimpering like a frightened animal. Nusti couldn't blame her—Nurim'isil was truly a sight to behold, and he wasn't entirely sure if this wasn't a dream.

His waking state was affirmed when Nurim'isil suddenly turned to Crina, who had been as silent as the others and, in a remarkable display of humility for a god, took a knee before him. The boy looked uncertain, but not scared, and Nurim'isil held out his hand. 'Turn around, child,' he said, 'and allow me to fix that broken wing of yours.' His voice was strong but gentle, and still carried the same warmth that it had before.

Crina's eyes were wide, but he didn't object; he did as his god asked and turned around, showing his broken wing to Nurim'isil. As Nusti watched, the god held his hand over Crina's broken wing and began to weave it back together with a power he hadn't seen before. Wisps of dark red magick wrapped themselves around the wing, and despite the seemingly brutal manner in which several of the veins snapped back into place, Crina showed no sign of being in any pain. The wing slowly flattened and returned to its former shape, and the glow of divine magick dimmed, before eventually disappearing. 'How does that feel?' Nurim'isil asked quietly. 'Better?'

Crina stood and flexed his wings, which spread fast and wide. He grinned, then turned and bowed to Nurim'isil. 'Thank you, Lord Father,' he said with a reverence Nusti hadn't seen from him before.

'I have merely righted a wrong,' Nurim'isil replied. 'A wrong which I should have prevented, like so many others.' There was a sadness in his eyes, and he turned to Paler'an. 'It has been a long time, *ima*.'

'It has been shy of *twelve thousand years*, Father,' she whispered. 'I thought I would never see you again.'

'And look what has become of you,' he replied. 'After *everything* that happened all those millennia ago...' He trailed off, his eyes growing distant for a moment, then sighed. 'We are back at the beginning, are we not?' he asked.

Nusti watched as Paler'an stepped forward with tears in her eyes. Her confidence was gone, replaced by shame and deference. 'Forgive me, Father,' she sobbed. 'I did only what I believed to be best.'

'And has that not been the problem from the start?' Nurim'isil shook his head. 'You are blinded by your love for your people, something that is normally such a noble trait. But your desire to shield them from either harm or change has twisted your mind to such an extent that you cannot conceive of a world that condones anything different.'

Paler'an didn't reply, but sunk to the ground, visibly defeated. Nusti stepped forward, nervous but uncontrollably curious. 'Excuse me...my Lord?' His Nascent was circling in a ring above him; it was behaving oddly, though that was understandable in the presence of a god.

Nurim'isil turned and gave him another warm smile. The change in his demeanour seemed at odds with the conversation he'd just been having with Paler'an, but Nusti ignored it. 'What is it, Nusti?' the god asked.

'I...I was wondering what all this is about. We've always been told that nothing outside the Forest existed, that it was all lost in the War for Heaven. Yet, the Lady Paler'an seemed to know of others, like the aelf that you appeared to us as.'

'Ah, yes.' Nurim'isil frowned. 'I expect this would all seem confusing to you.'

Nusti took a deep breath, knowing his next words would carry great risk. 'We've been lied to for long enough, Lord Father. We deserve the truth.'

IN HIS WINTER

U Ameril Umarol Osil

CHAPTER SIXTEEN
In Those Ancient Days

PALER'AN AND CRINA both gasped at Nusti's moment of reckless impudence. His Nascent collapsed to his shoulder again, just like it had when it had sensed his fear at the darkness under the Forest.

'How dare you, child!?' Paler'an snapped. 'Who are you to make demands of your god!?'

'Nusti!' Crina began to talk but fell quiet again. He seemed to be having trouble speaking in front of Nurim'isil, and Nusti couldn't blame him. A young faery, demanding explanations from a god? He himself wondered momentarily whether he'd lost his mind, until Nurim'isil bowed his head slightly.

'You are right, of course,' he replied. 'Much has been

kept from you, and the others of your race. Though it was for good reason, I believe the time is now right for you two, at least, to know the truth.' He raised his hand casually, and a cluster of vines burst from the ground beneath the group to form a raised circle around them.

'What is this?' Crina asked as he looked around in panic.

'Do not be afraid, Crina,' Nurim'isil replied. 'I could simply tell you what you need to know, but I think that *showing* you would be far more meaningful. You need to *feel* the impact of the knowledge I am about to impart.' Crina still looked unsure, so Nusti tentatively held out his hand. He didn't expect Crina to reciprocate, but to his surprise the other boy took it without hesitation, and Nusti smiled as he felt Crina's tension melt away.

'For you to truly understand why Paler'an is the way she is,' Nurim'isil continued, 'it is necessary for you to know what happened during the early years of the War for Heaven. It is in those ancient days that the seeds of your current struggle first took root, when Zar'aish the Destroyer plunged the world into chaos.' He waved his hand, and the Forest outside the circle of vines melted away into blackness, replaced by misty images of a world burning and bleeding. Aelves died, lands were shattered, and gods wept as Nusti looked on in shock whilst Nurim'isil began his tale.

'When the War for Heaven erupted,' he said, 'it spread across the face of our world in a tempest of death and destruction. The aelves fought to defend their countries, but the forces of Zar'aish contained beings they had never seen before: creatures of strange form and twisted power which our children struggled to repel. Each time the Dark One sent forth her forces, they contained new, stronger versions of those creatures, and as the war dragged on we *Imalaisir* foresaw that new races of our own making would be needed if the aelves had any hope of salvation.'

The images of desolation faded, and Nusti watched as the mists formed into a single image of Nurim'isil stood over a cot much like his own. Laid in the cot was a young female faery, and he realised with a start that it was Paler'an. He looked over to see a haunted look in her eyes; she was witnessing memories of her own creation, in a time before she'd ruled the Forest.

'And so it was that I gave life to your people, the *eraelvir*.' Nurim'isil spoke proudly, like a father. 'Paler'an was the first faery I created, and the others were made in her image. In those days you were one race, without distinction between the seasons. This Forest did not yet exist, as I had hoped for you to live in harmony with your elder brethren. At first the wood aelves welcomed the early faeries, whose ability to fly gave them a distinct advantage in battle.'

The mists shifted again, and Nusti beheld a great battle under towering trees, smaller than the Thronetree but still far taller than those that populated the Forest. Thousands of wood aelves charged through a forest as their faery brethren flew overhead, clashing with dark shapes that

Nusti didn't recognise.

'Zar'aish sent huge packs of dire wolves into the forests of the wood aelves, the realm called Isil'asir, and my two groups of children eventually defeated them by working together. I was elated that the wood aelves had taken their younger siblings into their home, and I believed a new time of prosperity awaited both your peoples after the war had ended.'

The misty images froze, leaving both aelf and faery suspended in time as Nurim'isil paused and looked at Paler'an with a terrible sadness in his eyes. 'Alas, it was not to be,' he said, and the elder faery looked away, unable to meet his gaze.

'What happened?' Crina asked with an insatiable curiosity in his eyes. Nurim'isil glanced at him, intrigued by his enthusiasm.

'When I first created Paler'an, I felt that she needed to have pride in her people if she were to lead them with love and purpose in the war to come. I instilled in her a fierce passion for the entire faery race, and it proved to be a great boon in the battles she led against the forces of the enemy.

'However, once the war had been driven from the lands of your elder kin, Paler'an changed. Her pride turned to arrogance, and her passion turned to unrelenting zeal. She came to believe the wood aelves owed their existence to her people and, given their ability to defeat the dire wolves where the wood aelves could not do so alone, she believed the faeries were superior to their elders in every way.

'Nearly forty years after the battles of Isil'asir ended, Paler'an led an uprising against the wood aelves in an attempt to supplant them.' The mists fuzzed slightly as Nurim'isil waved his hand, and when they began moving again the faeries in the image suddenly turned and descended on their elders, Paler'an herself leading them in a terrible slaughter. 'Aelf and faery clashed throughout the forests in a war that tore apart not only their peoples, but also my heart. To see my children killing each other, burning the dream that I'd had for them...it was too much to bear.'

Visions of countless dead, aelf and faery, brought tears to Nusti's eyes as he saw Paler'an engage a regal male aelf in single combat, wearing the same crazed look on her face that she had when chasing him and Crina from the Thronetree. He could only guess the man had been some kind of king, but he had no way of knowing for sure. He watched in horror as Paler'an swept the aelf's feet out from under him with a twisted spear and went to deliver the killing blow, but she was instead stopped by a brilliant light from the sky. Nurim'isil himself descended from the heavens in the vision, and Nusti watched as the god regarded the image of himself with sadness.

'Thus it was that I was forced to intervene,' he said. 'I stopped the war by taking the faeries and sequestering them away from the rest of the world.' In the vision, the earth split and twisted. 'I asked my brother, Bahul'tanar, to raise a ring of mountains around an area of forest that I had chosen to become the new home of the faeries. But...it was also to be their prison. Your prison. I could not bring myself to end the faery race for their crimes, but I was not willing to put my elder children at risk by letting them roam freely.

'And so, I changed the nature of what you faeries are. I split you into the four groups you know today and placed a limit on your numbers. Each group would be awake only during one season of the year, and you would only be as many as you have sleeping cots, to prevent Paler'an gathering enough faeries to attempt anything like what she'd done before. The nature of your existence is, I'm afraid, one of control. Because she betrayed my greatest hopes for her, and because I was too afraid for my firstborn children, whom I directed to set a watch on the walls of the Forest.'

The vision briefly showed Paler'an sat atop her throne, bitter and lonely, before it faded completely, and the Forest stood before them once more. Nurim'isil looked at Paler'an, who knelt weeping on the ground. 'In spite of all that happened,' he continued, 'I still had hope that she could learn from her transgressions, and that one day I could free the faeries from the walls of this Forest to walk amongst the wood aelves once more. Alas, it appears she still cannot abide that which is different, instead tending towards rash action rather than embracing reason and consideration.' He walked over and stood before Paler'an, who cowered back from her father.

'You care for your Forest and your people so deeply,' he said. 'It is one of the strongest traits I gave you, and why I was so proud of you once. But in your haste to protect it all, you resolved too quickly to send young Nusti back to sleep, when you would have been better served by understanding *why* he is awake. Once again, your choices have led to others being hurt, my daughter. Will you ever learn?'

As Nusti looked at Paler'an, he almost felt pity for her in that moment. The Queen of all Faeries, Custodian of the Forest, had once been her father's greatest hope.

Instead, she had become his most bitter disappointment.

U Airi Ihlais'hasha

CHAPTER SEVENTEEN
In His Winter

NURIM'ISIL TURNED TO Nusti, regarding him with a curious look in his eyes. 'Despite all she has told you, Nusti, you are not the *cause* of the darkness in the Forest, and putting you back to sleep will not remedy it. However, your awakening is a *symptom* of its influence, and I cannot say with any certainty that you will be able to return to slumber. I must assess your body's rhythm, to see how great the damage is.' He held out his hand. 'Would you come here, please?'

Nusti cautiously walked over to Nurim'isil and waited patiently as the god knelt before him and placed his hand upon Nusti's small chest. It felt warm, and Nusti saw Nurim'isil close his eyes in concentration. Silence hung over the group as the seconds passed, until eventually Nurim'isil took a deep breath and opened his eyes. 'It is as I thought,' he said.

'What is it?' Nusti asked.

'You are awake, young one, because the darkness has touched you. Though I cannot say precisely when, at some point during the last year it reached out and made contact with you. As a result, your sleep cycle has become severed from that of the Forest. Your ability to hibernate with the other gold faeries has been lost; if you try to sleep now, you will simply awaken when your body is rested. The original faeries slept much as the other races do, with the setting and rising of the sun. Without the connection to the Forest, you are returning to the natural rhythm that your body was designed to follow.'

Nusti swallowed a lump in his throat. 'So...what does that mean for me?'

'That is something you must decide for yourself.' Nurim'isil replied, eyeing him with a curious expression. 'I can restore the connection and put you back to sleep until Autumn next returns. You will return to your life as you knew it before, but...'

'But I would never be able to see Crina again, would I? I would never be awake...in his Winter.' Nusti looked longingly at the other boy, who was staring at them both with apprehension in his eyes. 'His cycle is intact?' he whispered.

Nurim'isil nodded. 'He is awake in his own season; thus his body has not been changed like yours. He will sleep once Spring arrives and awaken again next Winter with the rest of his people. I must be clear about this, Nusti: if you choose to sleep, you will never see Crina again.'

Tears began to form in Nusti's eyes. After everything that had happened, everything the two boys had been through, he was about to lose Crina. The bond that had begun to grow between them was strong, and the thought of breaking it was more than he could bear.

'Lord Father?' Crina asked suddenly, and Nusti looked over to see him locking eyes with Nurim'isil.

'What is it?' the old god asked.

'You said that you could restore Nusti's connection to the Forest, allowing him to sleep again.'

'That is correct.'

'Could you do the opposite? Break another connection?' Crina's voice was quiet, but strangely hopeful.

Nurim'isil allowed a hint of a smile to cross his lips. 'It would be difficult, and potentially dangerous...but yes, I could. Why do you ask me this?'

Crina turned and walked over to Nusti. The two boys stood in silence for a few moments as they looked at each other, Crina examining Nusti's face with a peculiar expression. 'Before you appeared in the Forest,' he said softly, 'my life was simple. I awoke, I did what I needed to and kept to myself. I was content, but...empty. I think I always knew something was missing, but I couldn't find it amongst my own people.

'And then you came, Nusti. You made me question everything I thought I knew and encouraged me to think differently. At first, I thought you were annoying, and someone to stay away from. You were breaking rules I didn't even know could be broken, and that made me uncomfortable. But as the days passed, and I spent time with you, I realised that you were just living life the way you know how. And I realised that I like the way you live. I like the way you see the world, but also how you see me. You don't see me as broken like the others do. When I'm with you, I feel like I'm...more, somehow. You're my friend.'

He took Nusti's hands in his and pulled them close to his chest, and Nusti saw that, despite his attempts to keep a stoic face, Crina had tears in his eyes. 'I can't go back to the way things were, Nusti,' he said as his voice broke slightly. 'I can't be on my own anymore, in this Winter where I wander alone and apart from my own people. The only place I want to be is where you are, and that means I have to be like you.' He turned to Nurim'isil. 'Lord Father, I think you know what I'm asking.'

The god nodded but held up a hand and looked at Nusti. 'Do *you* understand what Crina is asking of me?' he asked.

Nusti shook his head. 'I'm not sure I do,' he replied. He was shaking now, and not from the cold; Crina's fur was still wrapped around his shoulders, as warm as the day the other boy had given it to him.

'If the two of you are to remain together, Crina must be free to experience the world as you do now. The only way that can happen is if I break his connection to the Forest too, and allow his body's natural sleep rhythm to return, as yours has.'

Nusti gasped and looked back at Crina. 'You...you would do that?' he asked, his voice trembling. Their hands were still locked tightly together.

'I would,' Crina said with a smile. 'For me it's not a choice; I *have* to do this.'

Nusti nodded, blinking the tears from his eyes, and allowed Crina to withdraw his hands so he could turn back to Nurim'isil, who was still kneeling before them. The god smiled at the white-haired faery, then held out his hand to touch Crina's chest. 'This will feel a little strange, child. Are you ready?' Crina nodded; both closed their eyes, and a light shone at the point where Nurim'isil's hand touched Crina's chest. Much like it had when Crina's wing had been fixed, the light pulsed as Nurim'isil's face flickered in concentration. The seconds dragged on as the god attempted to isolate Crina from the Forest, and Nusti was almost beginning to feel nervous until, eventually, Nurim'isil leant back with a smile on his face.

'There,' he said softly as he looked at Crina. 'Your connection is now severed; how do you feel?'

Crina cocked his head slightly, looking at the floor as

though searching for something. 'It's...odd,' he replied. 'It feels quieter somehow.'

'The voices of the Forest no longer echo in your mind,' Nurim'isil replied. 'You may find it disorienting at first, but I promise you will adapt.'

Crina nodded, then threw his arms around Nusti and hugged him. It took Nusti quite by surprise, and it was a few moments before he thought to return the embrace. The two boys stood in silence, barely aware of the world around them, until eventually they broke apart.

'What have you done?' Paler'an's voice suddenly echoed through the clearing. 'Father, you have taken not just one, but now *two* of my children. What will happen when others learn of this? What will become of my people?'

Nurim'isil stood and turned to face his wayward daughter. 'You lost the right to demand an explanation of me when you put Nusti's life at risk, Paler'an. You might truly have believed that your pride in and love for your people was cause for you to betray everything I asked of you, but to deliberately put one of them in harm's way? You have fallen so far.' He paused. 'However, I will concede that the truth of what has happened here will likely cause too much unrest and disturbance amongst the faeries. Both you and I can resolve to keep this secret, but I must ask the two boys what they wish to do.'

Nusti and Crina looked at each other, a shared understanding passing between them. 'We don't want to stay here,' Nusti replied. 'Not after what's happened.'

'We want to leave the Forest,' Crina added, 'and see what the world beyond the mountains is like.'

Paler'an gasped, and stuttered as if to object, but Nurim'isil silenced her with a wave of his hand as he addressed the boys. 'You understand that if you choose to leave, that decision is permanent? To return to the Forest and leave again at a whim would disturb the natural order that still exists inside. The faeries as a people are not yet ready for the truth.'

The boys nodded, though Nusti felt a brief pang of loss at the thought of never seeing his home again. Nurim'isil seemed to notice this and rubbed his chin for a moment as he frowned in concentration.

'Perhaps...perhaps there is a way,' he continued. 'Despite Paler'an's failings, it remains my hope that the faeries can one day return to the outside world and live amongst their kin. For that to happen, there must be someone to teach them what the world beyond the Forest is like.' He smiled at the boys. 'If you are to leave, it is on the condition that you go into the world and learn as much as you can. Explore, meet new people, and experience what life is like beyond the mountains that surround this Forest. Then, in one hundred years and not before, you will return here to the Forest to tell the others what you have learnt. Do you agree?'

Nusti and Crina nodded excitedly, but Paler'an snorted. 'They will never survive the world beyond,' she hissed. 'It has changed too much. Besides, no faery can pass beyond the mountains; you made it that way yourself, Father.'

Nurim'isil shook his head as he reached out towards the boys. 'Even now, you underestimate me, child.'

Tendrils of green light burst forth from his hands and wrapped around Nusti and Crina, lifting them up into the air before they could react. The light coiled around them, slowly moving to their backs where it arced between their wings. Nusti felt his own wings tingle, and watched as Crina's began to grow. The change in size was not significant, and they remained the same colour, but he noticed that his own wings began to feel much stronger. As the magick grew to its peak, their wings glowed brightly, casting long shadows through the Forest. Then, all at once the light disappeared, and the boys sank slowly to the Forest floor.

'Your wings,' Nurim'isil said with a smile, 'and your bodies, are now strong enough to carry you over the mountains and beyond the Forest. You are now able to leave the borders of this land, like your ancestors could.'

Nusti flexed his wings, and they responded faster than they had before. He felt stronger too, as though the muscles in his back had grown. He could see Crina testing his too, and the two boys grinned at each other. 'Thank you,' they said in unison, bowing to Nurim'isil.

'No, thank *you*,' the god replied. 'Your bond, and the things you have achieved because of it, have sown the seeds of the future for the faeries. I have been waiting for this for a long time, and at last the work can begin to prepare them for reintegration. But there is one last thing I must do before you leave.'

With a wave of his hand and a flash of light, Nurim'isil summoned a figure into the clearing. Nusti gasped as he recognised the form of a wood aelf, though this one was female and dressed in white and green robes, with a golden circlet around her head. The aelf smiled at Nurim'isil and bowed—she did not seem surprised to be stood before a god.

'Lord Father,' she spoke softly. 'How might I serve you?'

'Athelar'si,' he said, returning the smile. 'I hope I did not take you from an important task?'

'None more important that being called to do the bidding of one's god,' the aelf replied. She looked at the group around her, suddenly realising she was in the presence of faeries. 'M-my lord,' she stuttered slightly, 'are we in *Shari'isil*?'

Nusti cocked his head at the name. *The* Hidden *Forest?* he thought, realising the implication of the difference in the two names for their home. *I suppose* Ainar'isil *isn't an accurate name anymore. This isn't the last forest...far from it.*

Nurim'isil nodded. 'We are,' he said, gesturing at Nusti and Crina. 'These two faeries will be leaving the Forest within a day. Please inform the sentinels that they will be passing the border, and that they do so at my behest.'

Athelar'si stared at the boys in surprise for a moment.

'They are leaving the Forest?' she asked. 'It..it is time, then?'

Nurim'isil shook his head. 'Only for these two. The rest will follow in time, I hope.'

The aelf paused, then bowed again. 'As you say, my lord,' she said. 'I am ready to return at your will.'

Nurim'isil waved his hand once more, and the aelf vanished as quickly as she had appeared. 'The way is clear for you,' he said. 'Go now with my hope, and that of your people. You have a century of exploration and experience ahead of you, my sons. Use it well.'

Nusti paused as a rustling sound drew his attention. His Nascent floated around from behind him, apparently having kept well out of the way of the godly magick being woven. He regarded it fondly as a realisation dawned on him. 'What of my Nascent?' he asked. 'What's to become of it?'

Nurim'isil held out his hand, and the Nascent happily bobbed over and rested on it. 'As it happens, this one is ready for rebirth, though it will undoubtedly have memories of what has transpired here today. It cannot leave the Forest, and we cannot allow it to pass on knowledge of these events for the same reason you are leaving.' He paused. 'The newborn faery it becomes will stay with Paler'an, as her ward. I believe she could use the focus, and I will be significantly more attentive from now on.' He looked at his daughter, who still appeared ashamed. 'I have stayed away long enough, I think.'

IN HIS WINTER

The two boys nodded, then turned to leave the clearing. Nusti could see the cliffs of the outer Forest ahead of them, and anticipation crept into his heart. They had just made their way to the edge of the clearing when Paler'an called after them.

'I'm sorry!' she cried, a pained look on her face. Whilst Crina didn't look back, Nusti glanced over his shoulder. She had a pained look on her face, and her hand was outstretched. 'I only tried to do what I thought was best. Please forgive me!'

Nusti turned back to face her. 'When we return in a hundred years, if you've truly changed...then I'll accept your apology.'

With that, he strode into the treeline after Crina, leaving Paler'an alone in the clearing to face the judgment of her god.

Am Urnahr Rulush

CHAPTER EIGHTEEN
The World Beyond

NUSTI STARED UP at the towering cliffs that bordered the Forest, wondering how long it would take to scale them. Crina stood next to him in silence, likely wondering the same thing. It was a strange feeling, knowing they were about to step into an unknown world, and Nusti was excited, if a little apprehensive.

He reflected on the events of the past few days, and how his life had changed completely in such a short time. He'd experienced Winter, and it had felt like another world to him. So much was the same, but just as much was different. The creatures, the trees, the flowers, there was so much variety. And then there was the people he'd met. To have met not only their queen and discovered her past, but also the very god that had created her...it was more than he could fathom.

It was Crina that had taken him the most by surprise, however. When he'd first left the Chamber of Autumn, he'd thought that maybe he might find someone willing to help him. Even when he'd first met Crina, he'd hoped for nothing more than someone who could guide him to some answers.

Instead, he'd found a new friend, and forged an incredible bond that he could carry with him beyond the borders of the Forest. It was still hard to believe he wasn't dreaming, and he looked across at Crina with a smile. 'Are you sure about this?' he asked, biting his lip slightly. 'Leaving everything behind, exploring the unknown? It's probably not going to be easy.'

Crina smiled. 'I'm sure,' he replied. 'We've got an uncertain and likely challenging path ahead of us, but I know everything will be fine.'

'You do?'

'Of course,' Crina said with a grin. 'After all, "no matter what happens, we can survive so long as we're together", right?'

As the other boy echoed his own words back to him, Nusti smiled. Crina had come out of his shell, and with it he'd brought companionship and reassurance to Nusti. He knew they had nothing to fear and, with Crina by his side, the world beyond the Forest would be one big adventure.

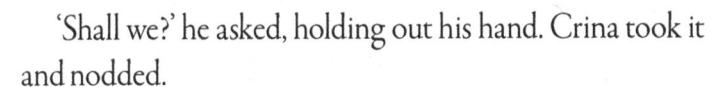

'Shall we?' he asked, holding out his hand. Crina took it and nodded.

'Let's go,' he said with a smile.

The two boys kicked off from the ground, propelled upwards by their newly strengthened wings faster than either of them had flown before. The cliffs raced past them, becoming a blur of brown and green as they sped towards the summit and the world beyond that awaited them.

They were free.

I Meleth u Ouri Cruhn

EPILOGUE
A Change in Her Heart

PALER'AN KNELT ON the Forest floor, clutching her head in her hands as she wept in grief and shame. Grief at the loss of two young faeries that she'd watched grow through the years, and shame that she was the one who'd driven them away. She'd forgotten what it felt like to question herself, to understand that she'd done wrong.

Nurim'isil stood over her, regarding her with an expression of pity. 'Stand up, Paler'an,' he commanded, his voice hard and powerful. She obeyed and rose to her feet to face her god.

'Father, I...' she began, but was silenced once more by Nurim'isil raising his hand.

'Enough,' he interjected. 'You have so disappointed me,

child. I truly believed you would have learned from your mistakes. I gave you *thousands* of years to consider what you'd done, tied your lifeforce to the Forest so you could experience the lifetimes necessary to understand where you faltered. It was all for naught, it seems.

'You became obsessed with protecting the Forest, so much so that you lost sight of what was truly important about it. You forgot the needs of your people and sought only to maintain the balance of the Forest, which in your hubris you thought gave you power. You have forgotten how much the wars consumed your people, and in turn, how they consumed you.'

Despite her shame, Paler'an did not look away from him; she knew her god demanded courage from her now. 'What is happening to the Forest, Father?' she asked, swallowing the lump that was forming in her throat. Nurim'isil looked away towards the Thronetree, and she followed his gaze.

'Nusti was but a symptom of a greater pain,' he said. 'He felt the darkness festering underneath the Forest, but he was not its cause.'

'Then what is?'

'You are, Paler'an.'

An icy feeling gripped her heart, and Paler'an felt her breath catch in her throat. 'M-me?'

Nurim'isil nodded. 'In a way, yes. This darkness...it is a lonely thing. It seeks that which is familiar to it. In your case, your close-minded attitude and determination to purge that which is different has drawn the darkness here to the Forest. It hungers in a way I have not seen since the Days of Strife, and I fear we will not be easily rid of it.'

'What am I to do?' Paler'an asked. 'How can I fight this?'

Nurim'isil looked at her, his expression softening somewhat. 'We will fight this together, child. You are still my beloved daughter, even if you have strayed from the path I set you on. But be under no illusion; dark things are happening in the world. Powers long buried are beginning to surface once more, and if you wish the Forest to survive what is to come, you will have to change and become something greater than what you have been thus far. If you wish your people to be free, you must rise above what you once were and face the coming darkness.' He looked up at the mountain peaks where two small figures, one white, one golden, were disappearing out of sight. He sighed, and Paler'an felt anticipation from him.

'We all must.'

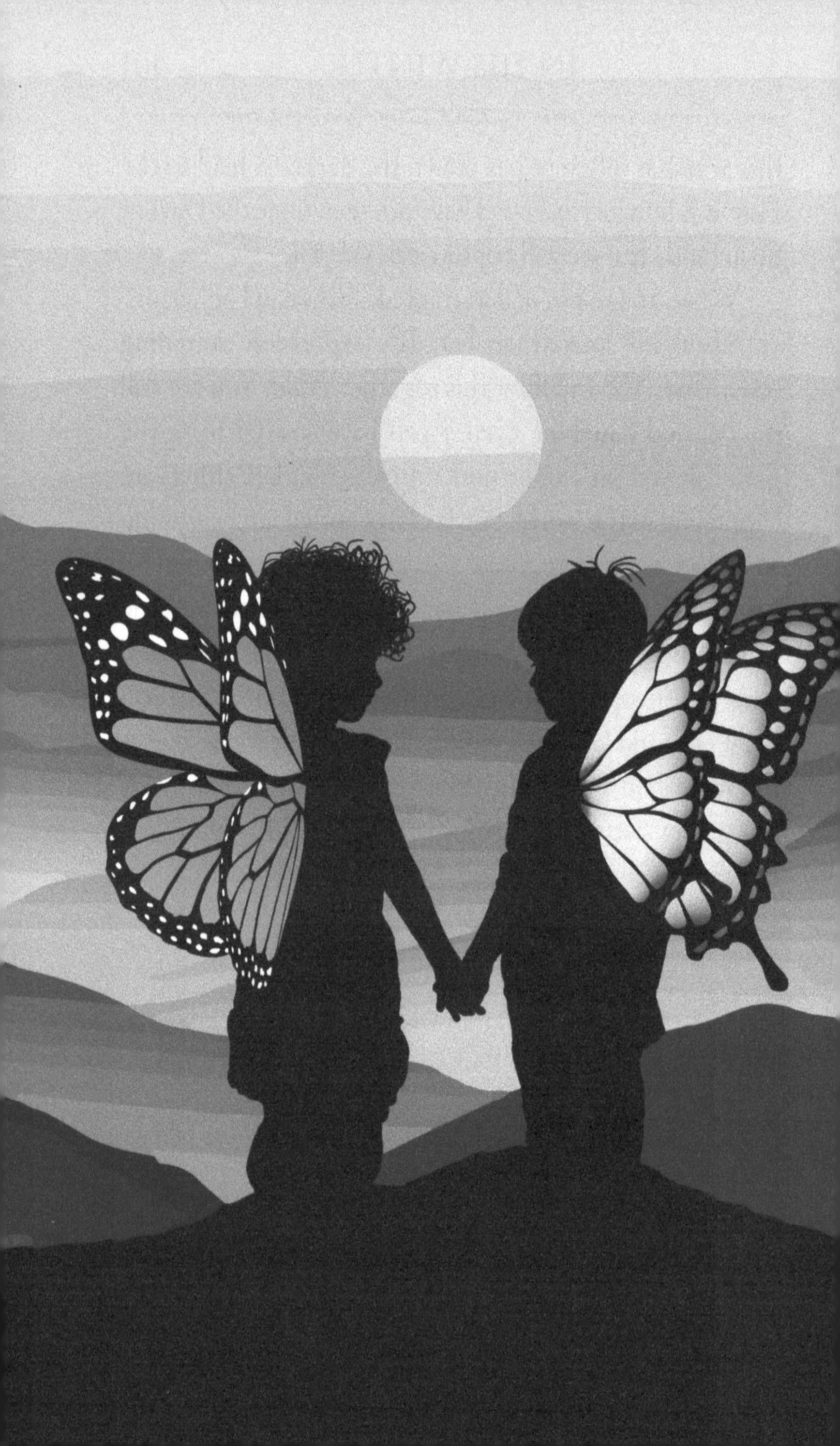

AFTERWORD

This book has been a labour of love. It's short, it's cute, and I adore the boys like they were my own children. If you loved it too, please do consider leaving a review on Amazon and social media, particularly Instagram – it's really important to independently published authors like me to get the word out, and reviews on Amazon are what help to get our stories to more people. You can find my Instagram at @author.rickysmith, and if you're reading this book then you likely already know where it is on Amazon!

ABOUT THE AUTHOR

Ricky Smith is an indie fantasy author who discovered his love for fantasy after picking up The Redemption of Althalus by David and Leigh Eddings in an airport bookshop. Twenty years later, that same copy still sits on his shelf as he pens his own stories, inspired by the legendary J. R. R. Tolkien as well as more recent authors like Brandon Sanderson, George R. R. Martin and Robert Jordan. For more information on his work, visit www.rickysmith.co.uk.